"I stuck to the truth."

His face crumpled. From across the table, she could hear his breathing becoming choppier. "Had I known about Chase, I would have found a way to stick around. You do know that, don't you?"

"Even with the threat of danger?" Violet asked, surprise evident in her voice. At this point, she couldn't say for certain what he might have done. She no longer knew the man. Maybe she never had.

"I would have found a way to stay here in town," Deacon insisted. "Believe me, I couldn't have walked away from the knowledge that you were carrying our child."

Violet wasn't sure if she could trust him, even though he sounded sincere. All of this new information was whirling around in her mind to the point where her head was pulsing with tension. In one fell swoop, she was finding out things about Deacon that had been hidden for a decade.

She didn't know what to think.

Belle Calhoune is a *New York Times* bestselling author. She grew up in a small town in Massachusetts. Married to her college sweetheart, she is raising two lovely daughters in Connecticut. A dog lover, she has one mini poodle and a black Lab. Writing for the Love Inspired line is a dream come true. Working at home in her pajamas is one of the best perks of the job. Belle enjoys summers in Cape Cod, traveling and reading.

Books by Belle Calhoune

Love Inspired

Serenity Peak

Her Alaskan Return
An Alaskan Blessing
His Secret Alaskan Family

Home to Owl Creek

Her Secret Alaskan Family
Alaskan Christmas Redemption
An Alaskan Twin Surprise
Hiding in Alaska
Their Alaskan Past
An Alaskan Christmas Promise

Alaskan Grooms

An Alaskan Wedding
Alaskan Reunion
A Match Made in Alaska
Reunited at Christmas
His Secret Alaskan Heiress
An Alaskan Christmas
Her Alaskan Cowboy

Visit the Author Profile page at LoveInspired.com.

HIS SECRET ALASKAN FAMILY

BELLE CALHOUNE

LOVE INSPIRED
INSPIRATIONAL ROMANCE

LOVE INSPIRED®
INSPIRATIONAL ROMANCE

ISBN-13: 978-1-335-90474-4

His Secret Alaskan Family

Copyright © 2025 by Sandra Calhoune

Love Inspired
22 Adelaide St. West, 41st Floor
Toronto, Ontario M5H 4E3, Canada
www.LoveInspired.com

Printed in U.S.A.

And when he cometh home, he calleth together his friends and neighbours, saying unto them, Rejoice with me; for I have found my sheep which was lost.
—*Luke* 15:6

For all of my readers. This one's for you.

Acknowledgments

I'm grateful to my editor, Katie Gowrie,
for working so hard on my behalf and asking
the deep questions about my characters.

Thankful to be partnering with my agent,
Jessica Alvarez. Thanks for always fighting for me.

And for senior editor Melissa Endlich.
Thanks for twenty books with the line.

Chapter One

~❦~

Violet Drummond stood on her family's property and surveyed the vast acreage, marveling at the number of healthy birch trees. The brisk April wind swept across her face, and she closed her eyes, enjoying the way it felt rippling against her skin. Whether snow, rain or sunshine, she loved the weather here in Alaska. Maybe it was due to the fact that she was a fourth-generation Alaskan—a native Alaskan but not an Alaskan Native.

This past winter had been brutal with an abundance of snow storms. Sometimes that didn't bode well for the birch trees, which were vital to the family business of making birch syrup. But, this year, not too much damage had been inflicted. She was thankful, and she knew her father would be as well. Abel Drummond had worked incredibly hard to get Sugar Works up and running ten years ago. Now, he worked just as hard to make sure it would become a household name and continue to be successful. She was doing her part as his second-in-command.

She smiled, thinking now about her younger sister, Skye, who had recently gotten married to Ryan Campbell, a childhood friend. They were raising their adopted daughter, Lula, and expecting a second child this summer. It was exciting watching them build their own house on the family property from the ground up.

Meanwhile, Violet's son, Chase, was a happy and healthy fourth grader despite the fact that he didn't have a father in his life. She had raised him on her own, which hadn't been easy. Despite a few hardships along the way, her family was so blessed these days.

She heard the sound of a vehicle's tires crunching on the road behind her but didn't turn around to see who was coming. So many work trucks drove along the path to Sugar Works, loading and unloading deliveries. The hum of activity was music to Violet's ears. She loved that it filled up the silence that sometimes caused her thoughts to wander to the past, a dangerous place for her to visit.

A car door slammed, followed by the shuffling sound of boots tramping in the snow.

"Violet." The deep male voice emanating from behind her caused her to instantly freeze up. It sounded so incredibly familiar, yet from another lifetime.

No, it can't be. Not after all this time. I must be imagining things.

She slowly turned around, immediately doing a double take. Violet felt a jolt coursing through her body as she laid eyes on the man who'd shattered her heart almost ten years ago. John Darrow. *Is it really him?* At six foot three with a mane of dark hair and a rugged build, he was just as striking as the first time she had ever laid eyes on him. Even now, he packed a solid punch that landed right in her gut.

"J-John? What are you doing here?" she asked, steadying herself from the impact of his sudden appearance. He took a step toward her, and she clumsily took a step back. She didn't want this man anywhere near her.

"Violet. I'm sorry for just showing up after all this time, but it's important that I speak to you." John's voice held a pleading tone, and his eyes implored her for understanding. She wasn't about to fall for it. John had always been good at getting what he wanted. She couldn't ever forget the way he had bamboozled her and then beat a fast path out of her life.

She shook her head in disbelief. "What

are you talking about? It's been almost a decade since you left. I've moved on. I think you should too."

"I know that I hurt you, but there's a reason that I left the way I did. I made a vow to make amends with all of the people I've hurt, and you're at the top of my list. You're also the last person I need to talk to. I've already spoken to my family and friends in Chicago."

She shook her head in disbelief. "There's nothing you could say at this point that I want to hear. You can skip over me and consider yourself done with your apology tour," she said, crossing her arms across her chest. "I don't want your apologies."

Out of the corner of her eye, Violet caught a flash of yellow and black. Her heart started thundering wildly in her chest. Down the road, the school bus was making its way at a fast clip along the path directly toward her.

Oh no! She needed to get rid of John before her son got off the bus. If Chase saw him, it would open up an entire can of worms. Her worlds were colliding, and she felt as if she might shatter at the impact. Her legs began to feel shaky like a bowl of Jell-O.

"You need to go. Now!" She ground the words out, leaving no doubt as to her feelings on the matter. All of her mama bear instincts were on heightened alert.

A look of confusion passed over John's face. For the moment, he had no idea what was going on, and Violet wanted to keep it that way. Protecting her son was her only concern right now.

"I mean it. You've got to go!" Violet said, clenching her teeth. "You can't be here."

"Just give me ten minutes," he said, an imploring tone in his voice.

Impossible! She didn't have ten minutes.

"Mom!" Her son's voice rang out as he stepped off the bus and ran toward her. Violet turned in his direction, smiling at the sight of her precious nine-year-old son. With his dark, curly hair, olive complexion and lanky physique, he looked so much like the man standing beside her it made Violet's stomach clench.

In a million years, she had never imagined a moment like this one. She had truly believed that John was gone from her life for good. But now, their son was hurtling in their direction without a care in the world. It was a surreal occurrence. She was tempted to pinch herself to make sure she wasn't dreaming.

"Mom! Wait till you hear what happened today at school," Chase shouted, coming to a grinding halt as soon as he reached her side. "I was nominated for class president. And I accepted. The election is in two weeks."

Pride filled her chest, momentarily distracting her from John's presence mere feet away. "Oh, Chase. That's wonderful news. I can't wait to hear your campaign speech." Her son had gone from a shy, introverted kid to everybody's buddy at school. It had been amazing to watch his transformation.

Chase seemed to finally notice John. "Hey! Who are you? I'm Chase. Chase Drummond." He pointed at Violet. "She's my mom."

John appeared startled for a moment, but he quickly recovered. "Hey, Chase. I'm Deacon Shaw, an old friend of your mom's."

Deacon Shaw? What was John playing at? Why had he given Chase a fictitious name? Was he hiding from someone?

"Nice to meet you, Deacon," Chase said with a grin that lit up his entire face.

"How old are you?" her ex-fiancé asked her son, his hazel eyes skimming over Chase as if he was studying his features like a book. She immediately tensed up, sensing his objective.

"Chase, why don't you head up to the house and start on your homework," Violet suggested, cutting off John's line of questioning. This was getting strange with John introducing himself as someone else and grilling Chase. She had no idea why he had shown up after all this time, but she wanted him to leave her family's property. "I left a plate of chocolate chip cookies out for you."

Chase punched his fist in the air. "Awesome! My favorite snack of all time." Before she could even say goodbye, Chase had run off in the direction of the house at breakneck speed.

Violet dragged her gaze back to John. He was staring after Chase as if he wanted to follow him. The intense expression etched on his face made her feel incredibly nervous. She swallowed past that feeling. She couldn't freeze up out of fear. She still needed to get John off the premises before the situation boiled over and became explosive.

"You lied to my son about your name." Violet's body pulsed with anger. "Such an unnecessary thing to do." What game was he playing? Honestly, she was beginning to wonder if he was a con man who'd come back to scam her. Nothing else made sense. It had been ten long years since she'd seen this man, and now he was back talking in riddles.

He probably thought that he could pull one over on her and then disappear as he'd done in the past. Little did he know that she was a changed woman—forever altered by their relationship.

She locked gazes with him, waiting for him to come up with a response. Violet couldn't imagine he had much of a defense, if any.

"I didn't lie to Chase, Violet." John's voice rang out, sure and steady. "My name isn't John Darrow. It's Deacon. Deacon Shaw."

Violet's jaw dropped. Deacon winced at what he saw glittering in her eyes. Disgust. Disbelief. In this moment, it was almost impossible to believe that they had once been head over heels in love and planning to live out their years together. So much had changed since then, yet Violet's beauty remained the same.

"What? You lied about your name when we met?" she asked, sounding horrified.

"Yes," he said somberly. "But there was a reason why I did that." Suddenly, after coming all this way, he was tongue tied. How could he ever make Violet understand the gravity of the situation he'd been in? It had been a matter of life and death for both of them. Being in WIT-SEC—the Witness Protection Program—had been full of dangers and pitfalls. It had been his refuge of last resort after witnessing horrific crimes and becoming a star witness.

She huffed out a deep breath. "Who does that? We were engaged. Was that just one big scam operation?" He could see the wheels turning in her head. As the daughter of a successful businessman, Violet was no doubt imagining he had been using her in some form or fashion. But he hadn't asked her for a single thing back then, with the exception of her hand in marriage. And that proposal had been motivated purely by love.

"I know it's hard to understand after all this time, but I had to for my own safety. And yours," Deacon explained. "Can we go inside and talk this over? I promise you, if we can have a civil discussion about this, everything will be crystal clear."

She wrinkled up her face as though she'd smelled something rotten. "Absolutely not. You've come back after a decade away with some wild story about having been in danger prior to your hasty departure. I'm not a fool, John…or Deacon or whoever you are. You left here like a thief in the night without a backward glance. You're not the type of person I want to invite inside my home." She paused to take a breath. "I don't even know who you really are!"

Ouch. That one hurt. Violet Drummond had been the love of his life. And she'd loved him too. Deeply. Clearly those feelings hadn't withstood the test of time, but he still respected her. He thought often about what might have been if he hadn't been forced to leave Serenity Peak.

Focus on your objective. Don't wallow in your feelings or the past. Be firm and strong. You've waited a decade for this moment!

"I think you've outstayed your welcome. Please leave…and don't come back." She was visibly bristling.

Violet's tone was downright hostile. He hadn't expected her to be exactly the same gentle woman he had known all those years ago, but she was so different now. He knew it from the hard edge in her voice and by the expression stamped on her face. This was not the same Violet Drummond. And it was all his fault. He had hardened her to life and love and who knew what else.

"I'm going to leave…for now," Deacon said. He really couldn't stick around where he wasn't wanted. "Whether or not you choose to believe me, I came here to make amends and to explain why I took off all those years ago. Hopefully, you'll allow me to explain myself once the shock has worn off."

"Don't count on it," she said, jutting out her chin.

A sense of frustration flooded him. "I can't force you to hear me out." He sucked in a ragged breath. "But after seeing Chase, I've got a host of questions to ask you, number one being…is he my son?"

Violet wasn't quite sure how she'd managed to get back to the house after Deacon's departure. Everything had passed in a blur once he'd thrown out the question about Chase. Somehow, she had gotten him to leave the property without answering him. She had watched as he'd made his way back to his vehicle and taken off down the main path. As soon as she had arrived back home, Violet had staggered to her bedroom and closed the door behind her so Chase wouldn't overhear.

She had fallen to her knees, sobbing and folding her hands in prayer. Her cries were born of desperation. Everything in her life seemed to be crumbling.

Please, Lord, help me find a way to sort through this mess without hurting my child. I don't know how to navigate my way through this storm.

She had never imagined being blindsided like this. Deacon had been out of her heart and mind for a long time now, only to come waltzing back into town.

After a few minutes of deep breathing, Violet left the solitude of her bedroom to check on Chase. As she walked downstairs toward the kitchen, she heard the low rumble of voices. She made her way toward the kitchen, listening to her father's voice as he engaged in a conversation with his grandson.

"You take after me," Abel said, pride radiating from his voice. "Science was always my best subject. Seems like it's yours as well." She watched from around the corner as her dad tousled Chase's curls. "You're a real whiz at it."

"That's the best compliment I've ever had," Chase gushed. "Maybe I can have my own company one day just like you."

Abel let out a throaty laugh. "If you keep working hard, anything is possible."

Chase took a bite of a chocolate chip cookie and washed it down with a large sip of milk. "Do you know if my dad was good at math?" he asked his grandfather.

For a moment, Abel looked uncomfortable. "Chase, if you have questions about your dad, you need to ask your mother. We've talked about this before, haven't we? It's not my place to tell you those things."

Violet raised a hand to her throat. Lately,

Chase had been exhibiting so much curiosity about the father he'd never known. She had always avoided his line of questioning, not wanting to lie to him but not ready to share the truth either. Violet had been aware that he had been peppering his grandfather with questions too, but until now she hadn't really felt pressured to come clean. It made her feel guilty and ashamed that she hadn't told Chase before.

If she hadn't been so foolish, she wouldn't even have let Deacon into her life ten years ago. But, then she wouldn't have Chase now, the best thing in her world. And she knew that Chase had every right to know about his father. It was perfectly natural that her son would be asking these questions.

"Okay," Chase said with a dramatic sigh, "but she never wants to talk about him. It's as if she hates him or something. Does she?"

"Sometimes things aren't black-and-white. Oftentimes there are shades of gray," her father explained in a patient tone.

Violet's hand rested over her heart. It wasn't her dad's job to field these questions. Without meaning to, she had made a mess of the situation.

"I hope that I'm not interrupting anything," Violet said as she stepped into the kitchen. She needed to rescue her father from Chase's nonstop questions before things got out of hand. Poor Abel shouldn't have to explain away her life choices to his grandson.

"Hey, Mom," Chase said. "Did Deacon leave?"

Her heart sank. Out of the mouths of babes. Kids were masters at bringing up subjects that grownups didn't want mentioned.

Abel wrinkled his nose and looked over at her. "Deacon? I'm not familiar with him. An old friend of yours?" he asked.

"Something like that," Violet murmured,

locking eyes with Abel and giving him a signal that let him know something was up.

A few minutes later, Chase threw down his pencil. "Phew. I'm done with my homework. Can I watch television for a bit before dinner?"

"Since you've finished your work, I'm going to say yes," Violet said, pressing a kiss to his cheek. "Way to go with finishing your homework so early."

Chase jumped up from the table and let out a triumphant cry. "Yesss!" he shouted. "Hard work pays off, even for a nine-year-old."

Violet and Abel chuckled as he ran out of the kitchen. Chase's antics always kept them in stitches. Her son managed to light up every room he entered, and he was the joy of her life. She would never regret giving birth to him, despite the circumstances being so challenging.

"So, what's wrong?" her father asked as soon as Chase was safely out of listening range. He raised an eyebrow. "I didn't like the expression on your face earlier."

Violet sank down into the chair next to Abel, taking a few moments to breathe and formulate her words. "Daddy, I just got the shock of a lifetime." She huffed out a breath. "John is back."

"What on earth!" Abel's tone was explosive. "Did you see him in town?"

She bit her lip, filled with anxiety. "No, he was here earlier."

Abel slapped his palm on the table. "He had the nerve to come here?"

Violet nodded, feeling a bit numb. "He approached me in the field with some story about wanting to tell me the truth about why he left all those years ago."

He made a strangled sound. "And Chase met him?"

She let out a sob. "Yes, he did. But the strange thing was that he introduced himself as Deacon Shaw. He told me that John Darrow had never been his name."

Abel's face turned several shades of

crimson. "I can't believe this. Never in a million years did I ever think that I could feel any worse about that man than I already did. It's bad enough that he walked out on you, but presenting himself as someone else is despicable."

Violet placed a hand on her stomach. She felt nauseated just thinking about the return of Chase's father. Her head was pounding, and her nerves were all over the place. She was trying to think of a logical reason for his sudden appearance but coming up empty-handed.

"There's something else," she said in a halting tone.

Her father reached out and gripped her hand, sensing she needed support. "Whatever it is, we'll handle it together as we've always done."

Tears slid down Violet's face. Her family had stood by her side when she had discovered she was pregnant with Chase, along with her best friend, Autumn Campbell, who had been a godsend. They had been supportive of her all these years as a single mother raising her son. Their love was unconditional. "Thanks for saying so, Daddy. That means the world to me."

She fiddled with her fingers, filled with so much nervous energy she didn't know what to do with it.

"Before he left, Deacon asked me if he was Chase's father. I don't think he's going to let this go." She let out an anguished cry. "Oh, Daddy. What if he tries to take Chase away from me when I tell him the truth?"

Chapter Two

Deacon Shaw left the Drummond property feeling completely overwhelmed after his face-to-face with Violet. Although his encounter with her had been full of tension, seeing the boy had rocked him to his core. It had felt like looking into a mirror when he'd gazed at Chase. Violet's son had the same dark hair and olive complexion as his own. Even his build was similar to Deacon's at that age. He didn't really need to do the math to tell him what his heart already knew.

I'm a father!

Unless the likeness was a total coincidence.

Even though it was possible that Chase wasn't his son, his gut feeling told him that he was. As a man who had been forced to rely on his instincts for the last decade in order to stay alive, Deacon knew his were on point. Violet's reaction had revealed so much. If he wasn't Chase's father, he imagined she would have told him in no uncertain terms. Yet she had ducked the question.

The last four months had been a whirlwind of discovery. After being released from WITSEC, he'd gone back to Chicago to reconnect with his family members. Tears misted his eyes at the memory of his reunion with his father, Benjamin Shaw. Their tight bond had never been severed, despite the lost years that stood between them. There had been a huge void at the family home without his mother's presence, but he'd found some comfort by visiting her burial site. Deacon would always wonder if his situation had contributed to his mother's illness and subsequent passing. He carried around the huge weight of guilt.

Pain rippled through him, reminding him that although he was finally free from the confines of the Witness Protection Program, the hits were still coming. If Chase was his son, it meant that he had missed out on nine years of his life. An eternity for both of them. Although he had returned to Serenity Peak to come clean to Violet about the reasons he had left her all those years ago, the possibility that he was a father changed everything. He couldn't simply leave town in a few days without exploring this newfound connection. In all the years he'd been in WITSEC, moving from place to place, Deacon had never been able to put down roots. No place ever became permanent. Yet, he might have roots right here in town, if what he suspected was true.

He shoved his emotions down into the

gaping black hole where he deposited all of his heartaches. It hurt too much to think about all he had lost over the years. He just needed to keep putting one foot in front of the other. Now that the danger to his life and the lives of others was over, he was being granted a fresh start. Finally, he was free to live life on his own terms. That freedom had brought him back to Serenity Peak so he could finally tell Violet the truth.

Violet Drummond was still the loveliest woman he'd ever laid eyes on. She was tall with an athletic build that spoke of hard work and discipline. Her long hair was an unusual shade of strawberry blond. In a certain light, it was fiery shades of red. Piercing green eyes and high cheekbones gave her a striking appearance. She wasn't a woman a person could easily forget. She was imprinted on him in all the ways that mattered.

Being back in Serenity Peak after all this time was a surreal experience. Although the downtown area had a lot of new shops and restaurants, the vibe of this small Alaskan town hadn't changed. It was still quaint and full of charm. Springtime in Alaska was a beautiful time of year with thawing snow and beautiful buds preparing to blossom. He hadn't realized how deeply the picturesque town had been imprinted on his heart until this very moment. Although he had lived in Maine and Washington state over the past decade, no place had stuck to him like Alaska.

He had made a reservation for two nights at the Forget-Me-Not Inn here in Serenity Peak. But now, he had to wonder if his stay would be extended. All he could think about was his son. Whether Violet liked it or not, Deacon was going to head back to the Drummond home tomorrow and seek her out. Whether or not she thought he deserved answers, he needed them.

As he drove through the downtown

area, he surprised himself by remembering the exact location of the inn. The establishment, run by an older couple named Clem and Patience, had always been charming. When he pulled up, Deacon noticed that the exterior had been spruced up a bit. The place looked like it had a fresh coat of paint, which made the sweet white Victorian with the baby blue shutters shine. A pair of rocking chairs sat on the porch, giving it an inviting air.

As soon as he stepped inside, the potent smell of flowers rose to his nostrils. He walked over to the check-in desk. The woman who greeted him was someone he'd met years and years ago. Sadie Whitaker, if he remembered correctly. She was related to the owners.

"Hey there. Welcome to the Forget-Me-Not Inn. Do you have a reservation?" she asked with a welcoming smile. With rounded cheeks and russet-colored skin, Sadie had always been a beautiful and kind woman. Sweetness radiated from her like a lovely bouquet of flowers.

"I made a reservation last week over the phone," Deacon said. "My name is Deacon Shaw."

Sadie narrowed her gaze as she looked at him. "You look familiar, but that name isn't ringing any bells," Sadie noted. "Have we met before?" she asked, frowning.

Deacon let out a sigh. It was only a matter of time before news traveled around Serenity Peak about his return. He might as well be up front about the situation. He had only lived in town for a little less than a year, but if he jogged her memory, he was pretty sure Sadie would remember him.

"Yes," he said with a nod. "Violet Drummond introduced us a long time ago. I went by John back then. John Darrow." He counted to ten. Deacon was pretty sure he knew what her reaction would be.

Sadie's face fell as recognition dawned. "Oh, wow. I—I remember you. It's been a while." She bit her lip as a look of worry spread across her face.

"Is there going to be a problem?" he asked, wondering if he was going to get the boot before he'd even seen his room. He really didn't have anywhere else to go. There weren't many inns or short-term rentals in town.

"Not at all," Sadie said, her expression shuttered. "I'm just going to need an ID and a form of payment for any incidentals."

He breathed a sigh of relief before giving her his license and credit card. After a few minutes, she handed him back his cards and key card, telling him, "Room 110 is right down the hall to your right. You have a lovely view of the Halcyon Mountains."

"Thanks," Deacon said as he accepted the room key card. He found his room easily, and once inside, he threw his bag down. Then he flung himself on the queen-size bed. What a day this had been, filled with travel and coming face-to-face with his past. He had known seeing Violet would be a moment of reckoning, but in his wildest dreams, he hadn't imagined the turn things had taken. Fatherhood had been the last thing on his mind.

He fought back the instinct to call his own father and tell him about this turn of events. *No, that will have to wait until I get confirmation from Violet*, he told himself. There was no need to get him all excited about having another grandchild if it wasn't actually true.

Within a few moments of lying down, Deacon felt himself dozing off.

Suddenly, a knocking sound jolted him awake from his restful sleep. Someone was at the door, he realized, probably Sadie. Perhaps she had changed her mind about allowing him to stay at the inn. Hopefully she simply had some extra towels to give him. But when he pulled the door open, he found his old friend, Gideon Ross, standing at the threshold, eyeing him with a look of shock, confusion and anger. So many emotions flooded him at the sight of his tall, broad-shouldered friend with warm brown skin and a big personality. He hadn't allowed himself to open up to many friendships during his years in hiding, and Gideon was a rare exception.

Deacon opened the door wider and beckoned him in. "I should have known Sadie would call you," he said. As a state trooper, Gideon was the one who folks in Serenity Peak reached out to when there was trouble. Clearly, Sadie thought he was a problem.

"I always tell my wife to call me if something unsettling happens," Gideon said, a frown etched on his face. "A man coming back to our small town after a ten-year absence using a new name falls under that category."

Deacon's jaw almost fell on the floor.

"Your wife? Wow. Things really have changed around here." Ten years ago, they had been broken up after Gideon called off their engagement. His old friend had always regretted letting love slip through his fingers. Despite his own emotional turmoil, it was nice to see that they had found their way back to one another. Love had conquered all for Sadie and Gideon.

"I can't believe you came back after all this time," Gideon said, his tone harsh. "What are you doing back here in Serenity Peak?"

Deacon winced. Gideon had been his closest friend in Serenity Peak, one who had shown him around town, taken him fishing on the waters of Kachemak Bay, bought him the best king crab he had ever eaten and offered him loyalty and companionship. In return, Deacon had unceremoniously left town without an explanation. Sure, he'd been running for his life and trying to keep Violet out of harm's way, but Gideon had no way of knowing that. Even though he'd been law enforcement, only the higher-ups had been in the loop.

He held up his hands. "All I ask is that you reserve judgment until I explain things. Will you do that?" Deacon asked. There was a pleading note to his voice that was born of desperation. He needed his old friend to be on his side. Maybe then he wouldn't feel like such an outsider.

Gideon folded his arms across his chest and locked eyes with Deacon. "Start talking now, John… Deacon, whoever you are. Give me one good reason not to run you out of town on a rail."

"You might want to sit down," Deacon said. "I have quite a story to tell."

"I'm fine standing," Gideon said. "And I'm listening."

Something told him he was going to be telling this story for as long as he remained in Serenity Peak. He hadn't really thought this through before his arrival. Would his explanation ever be enough to satisfy people?

"When I came to town ten years ago, it was because I was in the Witness Protection Program."

Gideon kept it cool, barely blinking at his announcement. "How did you end up in WITSEC?" he asked, his gaze narrowed as he regarded him.

"I'd been living in Chicago, my hometown, when I happened to witness a violent crime. Long story short, I ended up being a federal witness." At Gideon's silence, he added, "I was a target of retribution by the perpetrators. They were a well-known crime family in Chicago, so it was quite serious. If I hadn't entered the program, I most likely wouldn't be sitting here today."

"So was your identity compromised in Serenity Peak? I imagine that's why you left," Gideon said.

This was always the most painful part

of his story. Hurt rippled through him at the thought of his sweet mother, Rosie Shaw, and how he'd been separated from her as she'd fought cancer. Desperation had made him reach out to her via the telephone, but it had backfired big-time when he'd compromised his placement in Serenity Peak. Days after the phone call, he'd noticed someone following him in a dark-colored truck right before he'd been run off the road. The same day, a trespasser carrying a weapon had been arrested at Sugar Works. Every instinct had told him that his location had been discovered. He'd believed that, because of him, the Drummond family was in peril. Leaving had been his only option in order to keep Violet out of harm's way.

In the end, his mother had passed away while he was in the program, and it devastated him that he hadn't been there to hold her hand and tell her how much he adored her.

"Yes," he said curtly. "I messed up. And there was no choice but to relocate me."

"And WITSEC doesn't allow for disclosures to loved ones? So when you left, Violet was in the dark?"

He nodded, sadness enveloping him. He knew what his departure had done to Violet, who'd been his fiancée at the time. "Yes, I was forbidden from telling her about witness protection, and trust me, it still breaks my heart."

All morning, Violet had been nervous. She had sent Chase over to Skye's house so he would be out of the way during Deacon's visit. He was attending a birthday party for one of his friends, and her sister would take him to the bowling alley for the event. Gideon had called last night to broker a meeting between her and Deacon, assuring her that she needed to listen to what he had to say. Although she had been surprised by the call, maybe she shouldn't have been. The two men had been the best of friends back then.

When the knock sounded at the door, she answered it with a pit in her stomach. Deacon was standing there in a tan-colored light parka and a pair of dark-wash jeans. As always, he looked ruggedly handsome. Hazel-green eyes met her own, and for a moment Violet tumbled headlong into the past. Romantic picnics at the hot springs. Doing the polar plunge in freezing water as they tightly held hands. Deacon getting on bended knee to propose to her. Making plans for their future.

And then nothing but a hastily written note of goodbye. The proverbial rug had been pulled out from underneath her. And she had never seen him again—until yesterday. Violet hadn't ever truly recovered. Seeing her son's pain and confusion regarding the lack of a father in his life had gutted her. Being whispered about as an unwed mother had been stressful and demoralizing.

The only reason she had agreed to this meeting was because of her son. After withholding information for years about his father, the time had come for the truth to be spoken. But she needed answers first.

"Come in. I put a kettle on for tea," she said, leading him toward the kitchen. She still felt awkward calling him Deacon after knowing him as John. Violet wasn't sure that she would ever get used to it. Who was he really? She couldn't help but wonder.

Deacon followed behind her down the hall, and she gestured toward one of the chairs at the kitchen table. He sank down into a chair, making the butcher-block table look small in comparison to his size. She dragged her gaze away from him and busied herself preparing their tea. When she finished, Violet slid a cup toward him along with a plate of cookies, then sat down across from him.

"Thanks for agreeing to this meeting. I know this isn't easy for you, Violet," he said, cupping the mug between his hands before blowing on the hot liquid.

"That's an understatement," she said, letting out a brittle laugh. "Can we just get to it? You alluded to certain things yesterday that I haven't been able to wrap my head around. After all of these years, I'd like the whole truth."

Deacon nodded, his expression somber. "I've got a lot to explain, starting with my name. When I came to Serenity Peak ten and a half years ago, I was hiding my true identity. I was in the WITSEC program, which is federal witness protection."

Violet raised a hand to her throat. "Witness protection?" she asked, her voice ringing out with surprise. Although she had heard the term on a few television shows, she knew nothing about the logistics of the program. She wanted to pinch herself to make sure she wasn't dreaming this.

Deacon bowed his head. "Yes. Before I arrived in Serenity Peak, I witnessed some very serious crimes being committed. Two murders to be exact. At the business where I worked." He cringed, as if the details were being brought painfully back to life. "My boss was the shooter, and I soon discovered that the family was involved in organized crime. I reported what I'd seen to the authorities, and before I knew it my entire life was upside down. I was the star witness in a massive case that was plastered on every news show and newspaper. Not just in Chicago, where I lived, but all over the country. And then the attempts on my life began."

He ran a hand through his hair in a jerky movement. "They knew I was the star witness in the case against them even though my identity was supposed to have been kept confidential." He let out a frustrated sound. "The system isn't always designed to protect witnesses. After the third attempt on my life, the feds stepped in and offered me the opportunity to be given a new identity in a safe location. I agreed because I knew that those attempts weren't going to stop. I wanted to protect my family as well." He shrugged. "I figured if I disappeared they wouldn't be in the crossfire. It was hard, though, because I come from a large, tight-knit family. Leaving home tore me apart."

He stopped talking then, pausing to take a lengthy sip of his tea.

"This all sounds—" She fumbled for the words to express herself, but she couldn't come up with the right phrasing. Hearing this from a man she'd thought she had known was mind-blowing. And he had absolutely no reason to make up this fantastical tale since they had been out of each other's orbits for a decade.

Clearly, he was speaking the truth, and it was earth-shattering.

He arched a brow. "Unbelievable? I know. But in this instance, truth is stranger than fiction. If you need confirmation, Gideon checked out my story yesterday with the feds. It's all true, Violet."

"But why didn't you tell me?" she asked, unable to hold back the question. They had been so close, head over heels in love with one another. Or at least she'd thought so at the time. They'd even been in the midst of making wedding plans. "You could have laid all this out for me instead of taking off without any warning." Hurt was laced in her words. Clearly, he hadn't trusted her with his secrets.

He leaned across the table, his features creased with intensity. "I couldn't say a word because WITSEC forbids participants from disclosing any information about being in witness protection. Doing so can jeopardize the safety of the placement. I couldn't risk it. It would have put both of us in danger." His voice held a slight tenderness that she didn't want to hear. Although she was processing all of this information, she wasn't softening toward him. He had burned too many bridges between them for Violet to care. This meeting was all about Chase and what would be best for him moving forward. Her own feelings weren't nearly as important.

"So what made you leave town so abruptly?" She figured something must have changed in the situation to cause him to pack up and leave town.

He steepled his fingers in front of him. "I messed up. My mother had been undergoing cancer treatments before I left Chicago, and it was killing me not to be able to check in on her." The expression that came over his face was one of pure misery.

"So you reached out to her?" She imagined it would have been pure torture not to check in on his mother. Having lost her own mother abruptly due to complications from the flu, Violet knew the strong pull of familial connections.

"Yes, and it's the one thing they tell us explicitly not to do in the event that phone calls are being traced. The agent who was in charge of my case had reason to believe that I'd been found because of the call, and I was immediately pulled from Serenity Peak."

"Where did you go?" She couldn't help her curiosity.

He smiled faintly. "I ended up on Bainbridge Island outside Seattle. I stayed there for four years working at a nursery and specializing in landscape planting. Then I was relocated to St. Agatha, Maine, for the remainder of the time. It's a few miles from the Canadian border and one of the most remote places in New England. I was fortunate to find employment at a local arboretum."

"You were always good with the birch trees," she murmured.

"My heart has always led me to work with plants," he agreed.

Violet was torn between complete disbelief and acceptance of his version of events. Although his story was fantastical, he radiated sincerity. But then again, she thought, some folks knew how to spin a good tale. She had to wonder if she'd ever truly known this man. Yet, at the same time, she couldn't think of a single reason why he would come back after all this time to lie about his circumstances.

"So, what's changed? Isn't it dangerous for you to be here?" Violet asked. By coming here, had he placed Chase in danger? Her heart began to beat a wild rhythm at the thought of her son at the center of this mess. What if the danger had followed Deacon to Serenity Peak? She would never forgive him if Chase got tangled up in his mess.

"I'm not in WITSEC anymore, Violet. The threats ended when my former boss and his entourage died in prison. There's no one looking for me anymore. That's a fact."

She nibbled on her lip. Her heart was still beating fast. "And you're certain about that?"

"Absolutely. They would never have sanctioned my leaving the program if there was a chance that the danger was still present. The feds told me I could use my birth name and leave the program without having to look over my shoulder."

Relief washed over her. Deacon's situation had put him in grave danger. It was a blessing that his life had been spared. She was thankful for that.

"In the end, it was my decision," Deacon said. "I could have chosen to live out my days in witness protection, but that's not what I wanted for myself. Ten years was long enough." He drummed his fingers on the table. "I wanted my life back. Honestly, I think I deserved that."

"So your real name is Deacon Shaw," Violet said, trying out the sound of his name on her tongue. Although it still felt odd not to call him John, she was beginning to accept that his real name was Deacon. And he was from Chicago, not Boston as she'd believed. His whole profile had been constructed out of thin air. It was a bit mind-boggling.

"Yes. John Darrow was the name I was assigned in the WITSEC program. My true identity and back story was something I wasn't allowed to ever share, even with my future wife. I suppose that sounds very unfair." He locked gazes with her, his eyes full of intensity. "I'm so sorry for all of this, Violet. I know it must have hurt you terribly when I left and ended our engagement."

Violet swallowed past the huge lump in her throat. Words couldn't describe what she'd been through, and for so long she had hated him for deserting her. Finding out that she was pregnant with their child and that she would have to raise the baby on her own had been heartbreaking. She had been the subject of hurtful town gossip. But now, after everything she'd just discovered, all she felt was numbness. How could she be angry at Deacon for something that had been out of his control? He had been a victim as well. Yet she still felt angry that her life had been swallowed up by this entire mess. Instead of a wedding, she'd been in mourning.

Because of him, she had given up on the idea of love, believing it was nothing more than a fantasy. Her life had been in ruins. And it had taken her years to get back on her feet, which she'd done mainly because of her duty as a mother.

"It did cause me pain," she admitted, unwilling to get into the agonizing details. "But clearly you suffered way more than I did. I can't imagine having to leave your entire life behind and everything you'd ever known all because of something you witnessed." She let out a tutting sound. "Your poor family must have been in agony."

Deacon winced. "It was nightmarish for them. And even though I was able to go back to Chicago and reunite with them a few months ago, my mother passed away five years ago. I never got the chance to say goodbye." He steepled his hands in front of him and dropped his head down so she could no longer see his face. His pain was palpable. It hung in the very air around them. She of all people knew how devastating it was to lose one's mother.

She couldn't help but feel a groundswell of compassion for him in this moment. Clearly, doing the right thing and testifying against a criminal had seriously altered the course of Deacon's life. And hers and her son's too, if she was being completely honest with herself. Being in witness protection had kept

Deacon safe but it had also ripped him away from the life they were building. Because of circumstances outside of his control, Chase had been deprived of a father. Tears pooled in her eyes, and she tried in vain to blink them away.

"I'm so sorry for your loss, Deacon. I feel fortunate that I was able to say good-bye to my own mother before she passed. This all sounds so very difficult. I can't imagine what it must've been like to find out that your mother had passed away." Memories of her own mother were ever present. Sugar Drummond's memory hung in the air at home and throughout the vast Drummond properties. Sugar Works had been an idea Sugar had conceived of along with Violet's father. It was hard not to think of her impact on all of their lives.

Deacon swung his head up, and their gazes locked and held. For a moment, time stood still, and for all intents and purposes, it felt like she was looking at the man she'd once known. "Her name was Rosie, and she would have loved you," Deacon told her.

Before she could react, Deacon reached across the table and firmly clasped her hand in his own. She felt a tremor move through her hand at the contact.

"Violet, I've spent the last few weeks reaching out to the people I've harmed with my abrupt disappearance and the lies I've had to tell. I came back to Serenity Peak after all this time because I hated the thought of you believing that I deserted you because I didn't care about you…or us. That couldn't have been further from the truth. Now, hopefully you know that wasn't the case at all. I didn't have a choice."

Her mouth felt as dry as sandpaper. All she could do was nod. After all these years of separation, what could she really say to him? She had loved him fiercely, but life had forced her to move on from their relationship. Chase had become the center of her world, and she was no longer in love with this person she had once adored. She'd trusted him so much back then, but these days she was a little more jaded. Was this the whole truth and nothing but the truth?

She would need to check all of this out with Gideon before she fully accepted Deacon's version of events, despite the fact that she sensed he was being truthful. He had burned her once before, and she wasn't going down that road again. She would check out every last detail.

Suddenly, the sound of footsteps echoed in the hall right before her father appeared in the doorway with a thunderous expression stamped on his face. He advanced toward the kitchen table, stopping just as he reached Deacon's chair.

Abel glared at him, nostrils flaring. "I can't believe you had the audacity to come back to Serenity Peak after everything you put my daughter through. I think it's best that I show you the door." His voice rose with each word. "Right now."

Chapter Three

For Deacon, it was a surreal experience to be on the receiving end of a tongue-lashing by a man he admired above all others. Abel Drummond had been like a surrogate father to him during his time in Serenity Peak. Kind, loyal and trustworthy, Abel was beloved and respected by all. He had cried tears of joy upon learning that Deacon was engaged to Violet, telling him that he was the son of his heart. Clearly, judging by the fiery expression etched on his face, those days were over. And it hurt.

He stood up to greet Abel as a gesture

of respect. Of similar heights, they stood face-to-face, looking each other squarely in the eye. What he saw reflected back at him was mistrust and anger. At this moment, he wasn't sure Abel would ever believe a single word that came out of his mouth. Above all, Abel was a man who protected his family.

"Abel," Deacon said with a nod. "I know you're not thrilled to see me—"

"That's the understatement of the century," Abel said, letting out a grunt. Deacon wasn't sure he had ever seen his former friend so incensed. He couldn't say he blamed him. After all, he'd left Violet in the lurch all those years ago. And if his suspicion was right, she had discovered she was pregnant with his child after his departure.

Violet jumped up from her seat and went to stand by her father. She grabbed him by the arm. "Daddy, this isn't as cut-and-dried as it might seem. There's more to the story than you know."

"Violet, you're way too kind for your own good, and people take advantage of your kindness," Abel said, turning to face her. "Always have been, always will be too compassionate."

"That's not what this is about," Violet protested. "You need to slow down and listen."

"Abel, please hear me out," Deacon said in a pleading tone. "Believe it or not, I can explain everything."

"A decade without hearing from you speaks for itself. What could you possibly have to say for yourself?" Abel asked, throwing his hands in the air.

The sound of a throat being cleared caused all three of them to turn their heads. Gideon was standing in the kitchen doorway, dressed in his state trooper's uniform. Deacon couldn't remember ever being so happy to see anybody in his life. Gideon was a no-nonsense man, and he'd told Deacon that he believed his story.

"I let myself in when I heard your raised

voices from outside." Gideon turned toward Abel. "I think that I can help you sort this all out. That was my goal in coming out here."

Deacon let out a sigh of relief. Gideon was well respected in Serenity Peak, and he had checked out his story yesterday with the feds. Thankfully, Gideon was prepared to vouch for him. Hopefully, he would clear things up so the tension in the room would dissipate.

"If you think so, go for it, Gideon. I trust you," Abel said, shooting daggers at Deacon.

Ouch! Deacon thought. Regaining Abel's goodwill would be a monumental undertaking. He wondered if he should even try. Some roads in life were permanently closed to him.

"The man you knew as John Darrow was in the Witness Protection Program when he first arrived here," Gideon explained. "His real name is Deacon Shaw, and he was forced to leave Serenity Peak ten years ago because he was in grave danger. That's why he left the way he did and had no communication with anyone. It's part of the parameters of WITSEC. Not following those rules can be deadly."

"So you're saying that John is really Deacon? And he was in witness protection all this time? For ten years?" Abel asked, sounding incredulous.

"Yes," Gideon said, nodding. "That's exactly what I'm saying. I confirmed it yesterday with the WITSEC folks and my old boss, Tripp Baylor. There's no question that it's the truth."

Abel sank down into a chair and ran a hand over his face. "I—I can't believe all of this." He looked up at Deacon. "It's like something from a movie."

"Even now, it's hard for me to wrap my head around it as well," Deacon admitted. Losing a decade of his life to the criminals who had forced him into hiding had radically changed his world. He still had the emotional scars from the experience, and he wasn't certain he would ever heal from them. He didn't blame Abel for thinking the worst about him.

"I'm sorry for misjudging you," Abel said, looking chagrined.

Violet put her arm around her father. "It's not your fault. All you had to go on were the facts at your disposal. And they painted a terrible picture."

"We all came to the same conclusion, Abel," Gideon said. "And I think that's why Deacon's come back. He wanted to come clean with all of us, especially Violet."

Deacon nodded. "Making amends to everyone I've hurt is important to me. I started with my family, and now I'm here in Serenity Peak to do the same thing."

"Why don't we let Violet and… Deacon talk privately," Abel suggested. "I imagine you have things to discuss."

Deacon didn't miss the look Abel and Violet exchanged. Was this about Chase? Was Abel subtly acknowledging that he was the boy's father? He felt his pulse race like wildfire.

Just breathe, he reminded himself. *Don't get ahead of yourself.*

"Good idea," Gideon said, clapping Abel on the shoulder and walking toward the doorway in lockstep with him.

A silence descended on the room as soon as Violet and Deacon were alone. He imagined that neither one of them knew what to say in this tense moment.

After a few moments, Deacon said, "I'm sorry, Violet. For everything."

Violet's features were creased with strain. He hated being the reason for her frayed nerves. The last thing he had ever wanted was to bring more upheaval into her life. Over the years, he had beat himself up for bringing so much chaos to her doorstep. A part of him didn't even feel worthy to be sitting across from her at the Drummonds' table.

"I appreciate you saying that, but it's not necessary. From the sounds of it, you were caught in a bad situation with few viable choices." She nibbled on a biscuit. "You didn't do anything to deserve any of this. I hope you know that."

A feeling of astonishment washed over him. "I'm surprised to hear you say that. You were so upset yesterday when I arrived."

"That was before I knew your story, so can you really blame me for being upset? Ten years is a long time to be MIA with no explanation."

"It's a very long time," Deacon said in a low voice. "I imagine seeing me must have been quite a shock."

"It was, but I'm glad you explained everything." She shrugged. "Honestly, being angry at you didn't serve a purpose in my life, and I've tried to be intentional while raising Chase. Feeling angry just eats you up inside. It makes a person bitter."

Silence settled between them as he tried to come up with a tactful way to ask her about her son. So many years stood between them. Did he even have the right to pose the question?

Please, Lord, help me navigate this moment with a measure of grace. I want to know if what my heart is telling me happens to be true. Am I really a father?

Although in his gut he knew the answer, he needed to hear the confirmation from Violet anyway. Feeling as if he might be sick, Deacon forced the words out of his mouth.

"Now I would like to ask you a few questions, starting with the biggest one." He paused before saying, "Violet, is Chase my son?"

Violet let out the breath she had been holding ever since Deacon had approached her twenty-four hours earlier. There was no way on earth she could avoid telling him the truth. Not now after he'd told her about being in WITSEC and the traumas he'd experienced.

She was a bundle of nerves, and she wasn't even sure the words would come out right. Never in a million years had she imagined a moment like this one. She had never believed she would see Chase's father again, especially after all this time. If it had even been a remote possibility, Violet would have tried to prepare herself for this conversation. At the moment, she was flying by the seat of her pants.

"Yes, Chase is your son," she acknowledged, meeting his gaze head on. Her entire body suddenly felt boneless, and she wasn't sure she was breathing normally. And why was her heart racing so fast?

Deacon slumped back in his chair. For all intents and purposes, he looked like a defeated man. His complexion was now ashen. "I have a son," he said, shaking his head. "I'm a father."

"Yes, Deacon. You are. And our son is wonderful in so many ways. Bright. Curious. Charming. And very loving." She stumbled over the word *our*. She'd always thought of Chase as her son and hers alone. So much had changed in the last twenty-four hours. Her head was spinning.

"Has he asked about me? What have you told him?" Deacon asked, leaning forward across the table. He radiated intensity.

She fiddled with her fingers. "He's asked, but I've been a bit tight-lipped on the subject."

Deacon's gaze narrowed as he looked at her. "You must have told him something."

Violet heaved out a breath. The situation was getting more difficult by the moment. "I told him that you left Serenity Peak before you knew I was pregnant, and that I hadn't heard from you since." She cleared her throat. "I stuck to the truth."

His face crumpled. From across the table, she could hear his breathing becoming choppier. "Had I known about

Chase, I would have found a way to stick around. You do know that, don't you?"

"Even with the threat of danger?" Violet asked, surprised. At this point, she couldn't say for certain what he'd have done. She no longer knew the man. Maybe she never had.

"I would have found a way to stay here in town," Deacon insisted. "Believe me, I couldn't have walked away from the knowledge that you were carrying our child. It wouldn't have been possible."

Violet didn't know what to think, even though he sounded sincere. She wasn't sure if she could trust him. All of this new information was whirling around in her mind to the point where her head was pulsing with tension. In one fell swoop, she was finding out things about Deacon that had been hidden for a decade.

Violet picked up her teacup and lowered her gaze to it as she took a sip. When she finally looked up, she said, "I'll find a way to tell him. Give me a couple days, and I'll give you a call. We can arrange a meeting here at the property, where he can be most comfortable."

"A couple of days?" he repeated, shock registering in his tone. "I've already waited nine years. I'm not prepared to wait a day longer."

She bristled at his tone. "I understand your frustration, Deacon, but I think we both need time to absorb this. And frankly, I need to figure out how to tell Chase the news. He's certainly not expecting to find out his father is right here in town."

"Tell him the truth in a way a boy of his age can understand it. Explain what happened to me as honestly as you can," Deacon pleaded. "I think there's been enough secrets to last a lifetime."

A sigh slipped past her lips. "How long will you be in town? A few days? A week? I'm sure Chase will ask, and I want to give him as much information as possible."

"Violet, I'm not going anywhere. I'm going to stick around Serenity Peak indefinitely. Not only to meet my son, but to get to know him. We have so much time to make up for!"

A feeling of protectiveness washed over her. For nine years, she had been both mother and father for Chase. They shared a tight and loving bond. She didn't want anything in their relationship to change. With Deacon now in the picture, she couldn't help but fret over the new dynamic between the three of them. She couldn't ignore the fact that having a father in the picture would be a huge gift for Chase. Over the years, it had been obvious to her that he craved a father figure in his life. So many times he'd asked her questions about why all the other kids had dads and he didn't. She felt ashamed for always dodging his inquiries and giving him as little information as possible.

She swallowed past her fears. Violet was still reeling from everything that had transpired in the last twenty-four hours. "Okay, I'm open to speeding up the process, so maybe I can talk to him tomorrow. How does that sound?"

The hint of a smile played around his lips. "I appreciate that, Violet. I plan to practice what to say to him until then." He made a face. "I'm a newbie at this."

"You'll do fine," she said, trying to reassure him despite the churning sensation in her belly. "Just speak from the heart. Be genuine. Kids respond to that."

The sound of a door opening followed by footsteps echoed from down the hall, startling Violet. She could make out the sound of her son's voice as he ran upstairs.

Suddenly, Skye was standing in the doorway, looking frantic. "I'm so sorry," Skye apologized. Her blue eyes were wide. "Chase forgot his present and insisted on coming back to get it. I called your cell half a dozen times to give you a head's up, but you didn't answer."

Violet looked over at her phone sitting on the counter. She had turned the ringer off for privacy during her talk with Deacon. "No worries," she told her sister. "It's my fault for not checking. Chase is a pretty savvy kid. If you hadn't brought him back home, he would have known something was up." Chase was one of those kids whose brain worked overtime trying to solve riddles. He questioned everything under the sun.

"That's what I figured," Skye said, tears gathering in her eyes. She darted a glance in Deacon's direction. "Hello there," she said awkwardly. Violet knew Skye probably had no idea how to address Deacon after all this time. Ten years ago, he had been her buddy, someone she'd been wild about. Now, he was a veritable stranger with a dodgy track record.

"Hey there, sunshine," Deacon said with a huge grin, calling Skye by the pet name he'd once had for her. "I can't believe you're all grown up now."

Skye smiled back at him with a bit of uncertainty. She looked over at Violet for approval. She sent Skye a subtle nod, letting her know it was fine to engage with Deacon in a friendly manner. For all intents and purposes, he would be hanging out in town for the foreseeable future. Plus, he was Chase's father. There was no room for hostility between any of them.

"Welcome back," Skye said to Deacon. "It's way overdue."

Within seconds, they heard Chase's feet thundering back down the stairs, followed by the sound of shoes shuffling on the hardwood flooring. Violet immediately tensed up. She knew there was nothing in the world that could stop Chase from barreling into the kitchen like a force of nature.

"Should I head out the back door?" Deacon asked, standing up from the table.

Violet shook her head. "No, it's too late for that. Maybe I should just pull him aside and tell him right now, before he puts the pieces together on his own."

Chase ran into the kitchen with a gaily wrapped present in his hands, stopping short when he laid eyes on Deacon. "Hey, it's you," he said.

"Hi there, Chase," Deacon said, smiling at his son. "It's good to see you again."

Chase looked at Violet then back at Deacon, a puzzled expression stamped on his face. He frowned at Deacon. "You look like me."

The silence in the kitchen was deafening. Chase's observation had left everyone speechless. Chase took a step toward Deacon. He peered up at his face as if he was committing it to memory.

"Are you my dad?" he asked, his voice cracking with emotion.

Chapter Four

Deacon swallowed hard as his son's question hung in the air, like the aftermath of a detonated grenade. Skye quickly left the room so that it was just the three of them in the kitchen. He glanced over at Violet, who was twisting her fingers round and round. There was a beat of silence before Deacon took a step toward Chase and spoke.

"Yes, Chase. I'm your dad," he said, gently smiling at his son. Looking at him was like gazing into a mirror, Deacon thought. The resemblance was staggering. He had pictures of himself at nine years old that he hoped to show Chase one day. This kid was his mini me.

Chase's eyes widened, and he took a step back then looked over at Violet. "M-mom. Is it true?" he asked, clearly seeking affirmation from her rather than Deacon.

"Yes, Chase, it is," she confirmed, her voice sounding shaky. The Violet he remembered had been a cool and collected woman. At the moment, she looked as if she might jump out of her skin, not that Deacon could blame her. The situation was nerve-racking. At the same time, he couldn't deny the sense of excitement flowing through him. A whole new world was opening up for him.

Chase swung his gaze back to Deacon. "Where have you been my whole life?" He let out a sob. "I've always wanted a dad like the other kids."

Deacon felt a sharp pang in his heart. So many innocent lives had been affected by him being in witness protection. Chase had suffered more than anyone. A father shouldn't be a luxury. It should be a given in one's life.

Violet was openly crying now, huge tears rolling down her face. He knew that this was his moment to set things straight with Chase. It wasn't Violet's job to explain the situation.

"Chase, if I had known about you, nothing and no one could have stopped me from being in your life. But I left Serenity Peak before your mom knew she was pregnant with you," Deacon explained. He prayed Chase would hear the sincerity ringing out in his voice.

A look of confusion came over his son's face. His brows were knit together. "Why did you leave? Didn't you love my mom?"

His throat felt tight as he prepared to answer the question. "I loved your mom very much. We were planning to get married," Deacon explained, moving closer to Chase. This time, his son didn't back away from him.

Chase frowned. "She never told me that," he said, a hint of anger flaring in his voice. The last thing Deacon wanted was for Chase to be upset with Violet. She hadn't done a single thing wrong, and above all else, he needed his son to know that.

"What's important to understand is that I had to leave town because of a dangerous situation I was in. Your mother had no idea because I was forbidden to tell anyone about it." He let out a ragged sigh. This would be difficult for someone as young as Chase to wrap his head around, but he knew it was important to offer him a truthful explanation. "Years ago, I witnessed something really terrible, and the bad guys who did it were after me, so I had to change my name and keep moving from place to place."

Chase's eyes were as big as saucers. "What happened to the bad guys?" Chase asked. "Did they go to jail?"

"Well, not that long ago they were all

dealt with, and now I'm not in danger anymore. I'm free to live my life however I want," Deacon explained. "I came back to Alaska because I always wanted to set the record straight with your mother after leaving so suddenly. That's when I found out about you." He swung his gaze over to Violet. "And that's when I told your mother about what forced me to leave. She honestly had no idea."

Chase appeared to be absorbing everything Deacon had said to him. He didn't blame him one bit for taking his time. It was a lot of information to process! At some point down the road, he would give him more concrete details if he inquired. No more secrets, he vowed.

"Were you happy to find out about me?" his son asked. Chase looked as if he'd stopped breathing while waiting for Deacon to respond.

"Of course! I've always wanted a child of my own," Deacon admitted, "so I was over the moon. A bit nervous too if I'm being honest."

"Me too," Chase said, emitting a nervous laugh. "My stomach has butterflies."

Deacon laughed too. "I know this isn't going to be easy, but I want us to get to know each other. It might take some time, but I think we can get close. How does that sound to you?" His heart was in his throat as he waited for an answer.

"It sounds awesome." Chase said, his face lit up with excitement.

"I'm happy to hear that," Deacon said. And relieved. Things might not be picture-perfect as they worked on things, but he was going to do his best to forge a strong relationship with Chase. His mother would want that for him.

"Do you live here now?" Chase asked. Hope radiated from him. He was so innocent, and Deacon didn't want to do a single thing to disappoint him.

"Yes, I'm going to be living here in Serenity Peak for a while so that we can learn more about one another and form a relationship." Deacon grinned at his son. He couldn't remember the last time he'd felt this happy. He was finally getting a fresh start. And Chase was the cherry on top of the sundae.

Chase let out a gasp of delight. "So we can do things together like sledding and hiking in the mountains," he said, sounding breathless.

"Yeah, whatever you like," Deacon agreed. "I want to know what your hobbies are so I can join in and we can do them together." He was open to doing whatever it took to bond with his son. He would go above and beyond in his quest to make up for lost time.

Chase stuck out his hand for Deacon. It was a formal gesture, but Deacon understood where his son was coming from. As of yet, they really didn't know each other. They were strangers who shared a biological bond. He prayed that he could make inroads with Chase as quickly as possible. He had already missed nine years of his life. Deacon was determined not to miss another minute.

"Chase, why don't you go find Aunt Skye so she can take you to the party," Violet suggested. "There will be plenty of time to talk later."

"I can't wait to tell my friends that I met my dad," Chase said, his face lit up with a huge grin. "They'll want to meet you too."

"I'll see you soon," Deacon promised as Chase raced out of the room, present in hand. Deacon raked his hand through his hair and let out a sigh of relief. He sank down into a chair. "That was tougher than I thought, but at the same time, he made it easy. He's a good kid, Violet."

"The best," she said, blinking away new tears. Emotion rippled through her voice as she said, "He's been such a joy to raise. It's been the honor of my life."

And he'd missed every moment of the

experience. Guilt pierced his insides, even though the rational part of his brain knew it had been no fault of his own that he'd been forced to move from town to town. If only he'd stayed around a little longer, he would have discovered that Violet was carrying his child. Everything would have been different.

"I should thank you for that. You did all the heavy lifting by yourself." He stroked his jaw. "I get that being a single mom isn't for the faint of heart."

"No it's not," Violet agreed. "Everything considered, I've been fortunate. My family has been by my side every step of the way. They adore Chase." A hint of a smile played around her lips. "That's been a tremendous blessing."

Deacon nodded. The Drummonds were a wonderful family, loving and loyal. He had first been an employee at their company, Sugar Works, and soon he'd been welcomed into the fold as one of their own. He hated the fact that they'd all believed he'd deserted both Violet and the company. He'd loved her way too much to ever willingly walk away from her. Even now, just looking at her caused a pang in his heart. She was still the loveliest woman he'd ever laid his eyes on.

"I'm grateful for that," he said, hoping he would get the opportunity to express those sentiments directly to Abel and Skye too. He owed them both a debt of gratitude. From what he'd gleaned, his son was a well-adjusted and content nine-year-old. What more could he ask for under the circumstances?

"I've always been protective of Chase and that still stands." Her mouth set in a hard line. "And moving forward, I'm going to continue to protect him." Violet's statement hung in the air between them.

"From me? I would never do anything to hurt him," Deacon said, bristling at the implication. "I may not have been around to help you raise him, but I already feel a strong connection to him." He couldn't explain why, but Deacon felt an instinctual pull in Chase's direction.

She folded her arms across her chest. "Deacon, I sense your intentions are honorable, but let's face it, your life is a bit unsettled at the moment." Violet narrowed her gaze as she regarded him. "I don't want all of this to trickle down to Chase."

Did Violet think he was going to hurt their son? He would never do that! After all those lost years, he deserved to be a part of Chase's life. How could that be wrong?

"Neither do I," he answered, trying to keep his cool. "My goal is to enhance Chase's life, not complicate things."

"I sense you have the best of intentions, but this is a huge sea change for Chase. I just don't want anything to be disrupted. We really have to take things slowly," Violet cautioned.

Deacon shifted from one foot to the

other. Anger bubbled under the surface, but he took in a few gulps of air to steady himself. Violet was simply being a mother, but in the process, she wasn't being fair to him as Chase's father.

"Slowly?" he asked, his voice sounding raspy. He shook his head. "I'm not willing to do that. I've already lost nine years with him, Violet. Surely you can't expect me to lose a single moment more with our son."

They locked gazes for a few moments, neither of them giving an inch. The stubborn tilt of Violet's chin spoke volumes. He knew what it looked like when she dug in her heels. After all the years of being on the run, Deacon had finally thought he might find some peace in the process of bonding with his son. And now, Violet wanted to slow things down. He wondered if she really wanted things to grind to a halt.

"Just be honest. You're thinking I might hurt our son because that's what I did to you." He spit out the words, then pivoted to make a fast exit out of the kitchen. He knew that if he stuck around he might say something he would later come to regret.

After Deacon's hasty departure, Violet slumped down into a chair and put her head in her hands. Moments later, she heard the front door close with a slight bang. The last two days had been a whirlwind, full of surprises and lots of emotion. She was still grappling with the fact that John had returned to Serenity Peak as Deacon, let alone that he'd been in witness protection. And he'd known right away that Chase was his son, a fact she never would have been able to deny.

And now Chase had met his father, and his life would be forever altered.

So much had changed in a matter of hours. She needed to check in with Chase to see how he was processing the news, but that could wait until after his return from the birthday party. For the moment, he seemed all right, but once the news settled in, he might struggle with the revelation. He hadn't asked too many questions, but she knew there had to be some brewing in his mind. She couldn't help but wonder if he would press for more details about the things Deacon had witnessed that had landed him in WITSEC.

"Violet, are you all right? I just saw Deacon drive away." Skye's gentle voice drew her out of her thoughts. Her sister was standing in the entryway, a look of concern on her sweet face. "I dropped Chase off and came right back—I wanted to make sure that you were okay. Are you?"

"Honestly, I'm not sure," Violet admitted. "Everything is happening so fast it's making my head spin."

Skye walked over and sat down next to Violet. She reached out and squeezed her hand. "That's understandable. Chase's whole life is changing right before your eyes. Not to mention what you once thought to be true isn't. From what Chase told me, Deacon didn't abandon you. I know how much that hurt you at the time."

Hurt was an understatement. That period in her life had been incredibly painful. Violet had been gutted, especially after finding out that she was expecting a baby. And it had never really made sense to her that "John" would leave her the way he had. Now she knew why those doubts had plagued her.

"No, he didn't choose to leave me," Violet said, "but the effect is still the same. I lost the love of my life, and my son didn't have a father. I had to raise Chase on my own, which was the last thing I wanted for him. And for me." She wiped away tears from her cheeks.

"But he's back now, Violet," Skye said gently. "How does that make you feel?"

"My feelings are all over the place," Violet admitted. For so long now, she'd stuffed them all down, only to have them resurface with Deacon's return. She was mourning him all over again. "Honestly, he's a stranger after all this time. Not just to me, but to Chase as well. It seems as if it was another lifetime when we were engaged."

Skye reached down and placed her arms around her. She glanced at the wall clock. "I'll pick Chase up when the party is over. And I'm here for you whenever you need to talk."

"I appreciate that," Violet said. "Let me know if Chase seems upset or distant, okay?"

"Absolutely," Skye said, heading out of the kitchen.

Violet sat quietly in the stillness of the house until the sound of heavy boots caught her attention. Shortly after, her father entered the room. His boots were now off and he was only wearing socks. It was their routine to leave their boots on the mat by the door so as not to trek snow and dirt into the house.

"How did things go?" Abel asked, placing a hand on her shoulder.

Violet shrugged. "It's hard to tell. Chase is such an easygoing kid, so he handled it well, as did Deacon. I'm hoping he won't struggle with this moving forward." She worried that Chase would unravel a bit due to his sensitive nature. This was a lot for anyone to handle, let alone a child.

"That's good," Abel said, reaching into the fridge and pulling out a carton of milk. He reached for a tall glass and filled it to the brim before gulping the contents down.

She bit her lip. "I'm hoping he won't struggle with this new dynamic. His entire life, it's been just him and me, with you and Skye as backup."

"Well with Skye and Ryan getting married and adopting Lula, our family has been growing by leaps and bounds. Bonding with his father will be good for Chase." He shot her a knowing look. It had always been Abel's opinion that

Chase needed a strong father figure in his life. Although he was a devoted grandpa, he'd always insisted it wasn't the same as having a dad. And Violet had always known it was true.

"I hope so," she murmured. What was she so worried about? Maybe Deacon was right in his assessment. Perhaps she was worried her son would get hurt by his father just the way she'd been.

Violet sat up straight in her chair. "Anyway, what brings you home at this time of the day? I thought you were collecting specimens from some of the birch trees."

"I was." Abel knit his brows together. "I know you've got a lot on your plate, but I have some bad news."

"Oh, no! What happened?" Violet asked, bracing for the worst. Her father wasn't one to exaggerate. He dealt with situations calmly and with pragmatism. She could tell by his expression that something serious was brewing. And she sensed it was related to Sugar Works.

"A whole section of trees are showing signs of disease. Out in the southern portion," he explained.

As a company that depended on healthy birch trees to make birch syrup, this news was alarming. "How bad is it?"

"So far it's fairly contained, but we've got to make sure all hands are on deck. These outbreaks can escalate fairly quickly if they're not mitigated."

"Can we save the infected trees?" she asked. It wasn't always possible. While losing trees for any reason was painful, diseased ones led to fears of the problem spreading.

"I'm praying we can. I've got a call in to Clyde, and I'm hoping he gets back to me soon." Although Abel was trying to hide it, Violet could hear the concern laced in his voice. Sugar Works was entering its most productive season. This could be disastrous for tapping the birch trees and making their popular product.

The company was officially coming into its own after years of struggle.

She was happy that her father had reached out for assistance. Clyde Brown was a local arborist whom Abel had consulted with over the years when there was trouble with the birch trees. He was a skilled professional who knew everything about Alaskan trees. Getting his input would be invaluable.

Violet stood up and hugged Abel. "Everything will be fine. I'm going to get my gear on and head over there to check things out."

"I can always count on you, can't I? I'm not sure what I would do without you, Violet." His voice trembled. "You've done so much to make Sugar Works a success."

"You know I love our company. Along with Chase, it's given my life a purpose." And she had needed one after her life had been torn apart. All of her plans had been in ruins after Deacon's departure.

She was proud of making lemonade out of lemons.

"Your life always had purpose, ever since you were a small girl. I know you thought you would take another path, but I couldn't be any prouder of the woman you've become." Abel's voice was loaded with emotion.

Her father knew better than anyone how she had been forced to abandon her dreams of a life with Deacon. By leaning on God and clinging to her faith, she had dried her tears, redirected herself and crafted a new life for herself.

And even though Deacon was back in Serenity Peak and eager to reclaim the life he'd sacrificed, she wasn't going to allow him to turn her orderly life into chaos.

Chapter Five

Deacon drove away from Violet and the Drummond home as fast as he possibly could without being reckless. As he navigated the twisting roads, the expansive property stretched out before him, instantly calming him down. There were beautiful birch trees as far as the eye could see. He spotted a majestic eagle swooping down to capture its prey. Memories washed over him, transporting him back in time to when he'd begun working for Abel Drummond at Sugar Works. Due to his experience as an arborist, he'd been hired the very moment he had shown up at the property looking for work. At only twenty-seven years old, he had been grateful for the opportunity to work for such a wonderful company.

And then he had met Violet. Deacon had known the moment he'd laid eyes on her that she was going to be someone special in his life. And she had been the woman of his dreams, someone he'd wanted to walk through life alongside. She had been some kind of wonderful, the type of woman a man couldn't forget.

She was just as lovely today as she'd been all those years ago. And despite the years that stretched out between them, being in her presence still made pure adrenaline race through his veins. He didn't want to examine his feelings too closely. Too much time had elapsed for him to ever pursue anything romantic with Violet. His focus needed to stay on his son. He couldn't allow the past to have such a stranglehold on him.

Not that he would even have a chance

with Violet. She clearly was struggling with the fact that he'd turned up in Alaska.

As if on autopilot, he headed back into town, heading instinctively toward Northern Lights, one of his favorite spots in Serenity Peak. The establishment sat on a cliff overlooking the stunning waters of Kachemak Bay. Once he stepped out of the truck, Deacon stood and gazed down at the water, taking a deep breath of the pristine air. The sight of the Halcyon Mountains in the background was majestic and awe-inspiring. He almost wanted to pinch himself to make sure that he wasn't dreaming. Being in Serenity Peak didn't seem real after all the years he'd spent fantasizing about coming back to this place he adored.

Owned by Sean Hines, a former football player turned restauranteur, Northern Lights was known for its award-winning cuisine. Popular and beloved by all the townsfolk, Sean had been a buddy of his during the time he'd spent in Serenity

Peak. It was a bit strange walking into the establishment without knowing how he would be received by his old friend. Not to mention the townsfolk. He knew gossip flew on the wind in small towns, and his return was perfect fodder for chatter.

Taking a deep breath to steady himself, Deacon headed inside.

As soon as he walked into the restaurant, the delicious aroma of grilled seafood greeted him. His stomach rumbled in appreciation. At this moment, there was nothing he wanted more than a platter of shrimp and crab legs. All of the seafood was fresh from the bay, something Sean had always prided himself on. Deacon looked around the place, noticing a handful of patrons giving him glances he wouldn't categorize as friendly. But they weren't outwardly hostile, he realized. He imagined they were simply curious about his return.

Within seconds, he spotted Sean chopping it up with a few customers, his head thrown back in laughter. As always, he was Mr. Personality. With an athletic physique and warm brown skin, Sean was the type of man who stood out in any situation. Deacon watched as Sean swung his gaze in his direction and slowly walked toward him.

"I heard you were back," Sean said, eyeing him warily. "But now you're going by another name. Have I got that right?" he asked.

"Deacon is my given name," he said with a nod. "Deacon Shaw. And I'm not sure what else you heard, but I didn't leave voluntarily. Please let me know if I'm welcome here or not," Deacon said, prepared to leave if need be. So far his reception in Serenity Peak had been a mixed bag. He had the feeling folks didn't know what to think about his disappearing act and subsequent return. He prayed that Sean didn't object to his presence at his eatery. He'd always been open-minded in the past. All Deacon wanted was a fair chance. And he didn't want his son to be the subject of any town talk due to his actions.

"Care to tell me the details? I never understood why you left Serenity Peak. The way you used to look at Violet was telling." Sean shook his head. "You loved her. Of that I'm sure. I believe you when you say it was against your will. Nothing else makes sense to me."

He let out a sigh of relief. It felt nice to be given the benefit of the doubt. Even though he hadn't done anything to create the situation he'd found himself in, Deacon still felt guilty about the fallout. Hurting people never felt good. Because of him, so many lives had been turned upside down.

"Why don't we talk in private," Sean suggested, leading him to his office in the back. Once they were inside, Sean shut the door behind him and gestured toward a vacant chair. He leaned against his own desk, facing Deacon.

"So, talk to me," Sean said, getting right to it.

"I was a witness to a crime back in Chicago, which is my hometown. I won't bog you down with all the details, but I found employment with a shady crime family when I was twenty-two years old. That's how this whole mess started." He let out a brittle laugh. "I was young and foolish. All I was focused on was making fast money. I worked for them for a few years, not realizing what was going on. By the time I understood, every instinct told me that I was in over my head. And the situation became explosive when I witnessed two people being murdered. Once I became a federal witness, my life was in danger." He shrugged. "Even after the trial, I was a target for retribution, so I entered witness protection and came to Serenity Peak with a new name and a new story so I could become anonymous."

Sean looked at him with big eyes and

let out a low whistle. "Now that's some kind of story."

He quirked his mouth. "It happens to be the truth."

"Sorry," Sean said, a look of regret etched on his face. "I didn't mean to doubt you. What made you leave town after you settled here?"

"I called my mom, which breached the rules of WITSEC—and it's how I was found. A few frightening incidents occurred as a result of that breach. They sent folks to come find me. It was no longer a safe situation for me...or Violet," he explained. "Now I'm no longer in the Witness Protection Program since the crime organization is out of business, so to speak."

"If anyone else came in here and told me that story, I'd bounce them right out of here, but I believe you. You were always a straight shooter," Sean said, reaching out and shaking Deacon's hand. "I'm sorry for what you've been through."

Deacon let out the breath he'd been holding. It was awkward retelling his story so many times, but Sean accepting him at his word was an amazing feeling. It was nice to have a friend in town. "Thanks, Sean. You might be the only person who believed my story right off the bat. Violet took some convincing."

"The two of you were the real deal," Sean said, stroking his jaw. "From what I remember, she was pretty broken up about your leaving town." Sean shrugged. "She refused to talk about it, though, after the initial shock wore off."

Deacon didn't know how to respond. Talking about his past with Violet was painful, and he hated that his actions had hurt her. The memories were bittersweet because of all he'd lost. In a perfect world, he would have stayed in Alaska, married Violet and raised Chase with her. But, as he had learned over and over again, life wasn't fair. At least not in his experience.

Sean placed his arm on Deacon's shoulder. "I appreciate you sharing this with me. It can't be easy coming back after all this time has gone by."

It had been difficult for him to open up to folks after he'd left Serenity Peak and Violet. In the ensuing years, he'd struggled to make meaningful connections, knowing he might have to up and leave his location again. Confiding in Sean felt like a step forward. Speaking openly about WITSEC made him feel as if a weight had been lifted off his shoulders.

"No, it isn't easy, but finding out about my son is a great incentive to stick around to get to know him." As he spoke, there was a little hitch in his heart. Chase was his son, and he wasn't going to let anyone or anything get in the way of their budding relationship.

"He's an amazing kid, as you'll soon find out," Sean said, grinning. "Let's go order you a nice seafood lunch. On the house."

"That's not necessary," Deacon said. The last thing he wanted was to be an object of pity. He still had his pride, after all.

"Come on. It'll be a welcome back to Serenity Peak gift." Sean pointed at him. "Next time, you're definitely paying."

"Okay then. I'll take you up on that offer," Deacon said, chuckling along with his old friend as he led the way back to the main dining area.

It was the first time he'd laughed so freely since being back in town. Although he had a lot on his mind, he was happy that he had some support in Serenity Peak. Sean would be a great ally. Being in witness protection had been a lonely road to travel. He had made a few friends over the years, particularly in Maine, but he'd always kept them at arm's length. And it had been difficult for him to rid himself of the guilt he carried around regarding Violet and his family. Though he'd dated here and there, Deacon had never laid his heart on the line again with any woman. How could he ever have cultivated a serious relationship after what he'd done to Violet?

Hopefully this new chapter of his life would be filled with better days.

For the past twenty-four hours, Violet had been knee-deep in work, so much so that she'd barely seen her son. It wasn't ideal considering they needed to talk about Deacon, but the situation with the birch trees was dire. With Clyde's assistance, they had been able to make a determination that bronze birch borers, a species of beetle larvae, were the culprits. These insects burrowed underneath the bark and infested the trees. They needed to act quickly to save as many trees as possible and to prevent the situation from worsening. If it did, the damage could be extensive.

They had assembled as many of their workers as possible, but several of them were out sick with a stomach virus spreading around town. Frankly, the virus couldn't have come at a worse time. At the moment, Violet and her father were taking a quick lunch break at the house and formulating the best way to handle the situation while being short staffed. She had quickly heated up some leftovers in the microwave, then doled out servings for both of them.

"I feel guilty even taking a break," Abel muttered. "Time's a wasting."

"Now, you know it's important to nourish our bodies so we can keep our strength up," Violet said, repeating her father's words back to him. How many times had he told her and Skye the very same thing over the years?

"When it rains, it pours," Abel said, deep wrinkles forming on his forehead. "In addition to the diseased trees, this stomach bug has affected a fair amount of our employees. Clyde called me earlier. He's sick too."

"Which means they can't help out in this crisis," Violet said, sucking in a deep breath. "Is there any way we could bring in some workers from neighboring areas like Homer or Owl Creek?" Time was of the essence. If they waited, things could spiral in a bad direction.

"I have some calls in now, but in the meantime, I have an idea that might help us out," Abel said. A strange expression sat on his face that she couldn't read.

"Okay," she said, waiting for him to elaborate. The way he paused made the hairs on the back of her neck tingle. *What is he up to?* she wondered. She knew this man like the back of her hand, and something was going on.

"Deacon used to work for us," Abel said. "We could use someone like him right about now."

Violet dropped her spoon down in her bowl, making a large clanking sound in the process. "Deacon?" she asked, her voice raised. "You want him to work with us?"

"Hear me out, Violet. Deacon was a wonderful employee, and he's really knowledgeable about trees. The last time we had this issue, he helped out tremendously. It's a no-brainer."

He was right! Deacon had been an exemplary employee for Sugar Works. Not only had he been reliable and knowledgeable, but he had truly loved the work. How many times had he said that working for Sugar Works was his dream job? But still...

"I don't think it's a good idea," she blurted.

"What's your issue with it?" he asked, frowning. "Based on everything we've learned, he didn't just up and leave you on a whim. Sounds like he didn't have a choice. The odds have been stacked against him for so long. He deserves a break, if you ask me. And we need all the help we can get."

She understood that Deacon had been in an impossible position back then. But

in the here and now, she was still struggling to find a way to co-parent with him.
It all felt incredibly awkward. Working
in close proximity to him seemed like a
recipe for disaster.

"Deacon and I fell for each other working alongside one another," she said,
shrugging. "It might be uncomfortable."
She wasn't quite sure why the idea of
working with Deacon unsettled her so
much, but she imagined it was because
she no longer knew him. Ages ago she
had filed him away as nothing more than
a memory, only to have him resurface.
They had enjoyed a whirlwind courtship,
becoming engaged after six months of
dating. Deacon had only lived in town for
eleven months before his abrupt departure. He had worked for Sugar Works the
entire time, having been hired by Abel
shortly after his arrival.

"I understand," Abel said, reaching out
and patting her hand. "I shouldn't have
asked. I just figured now that he's going

to be a fixture in Chase's life—" his voice trailed off. He was gazing at her with such a look of disappointment in his eyes it made her feel awful.

What am I doing? They urgently needed help due to the destruction of the birch trees and their sick workers. How could she justify not utilizing the services of someone like Deacon? It would be incredibly selfish, and there really wasn't any reason for her to draw a line in the sand. Not to mention their son was eager to connect with his father. Perhaps a position at Sugar Works would anchor him to Serenity Peak and give Chase a better shot at having a relationship with Deacon.

Be the better person. The phrase, commonly used by her mother, came to mind. "Fine," she said at last. "I'm okay with asking Deacon to help out."

"If you're sure about this, I'll reach out to him," her father said, letting out a sigh of relief. Violet knew how worried he was, and she wanted to do everything possible to ease his burdens. This would be a start. They still needed more staff to fill in the gaps.

"No, it should be me," Violet said. "I have to pick up Chase early from school, so I can swing by the inn and ask him in person."

Abel grinned. "Have I told you lately what a great daughter you are?" he asked.

"Not nearly often enough," she said, chuckling. "I won't tell Skye that I'm your favorite," Violet teased. She knew that their father loved them both equally. He was a man who had plenty of love to go around for the whole family.

After lunch, Violet headed into town, with her first stop being the Forget-Me-Not Inn. The drive allowed her to mellow out while listening to pop songs on the radio. Music was always good for the soul, and at the moment, she needed the lightness amidst all the unfolding drama. She was still trying to wrap her head around Deacon's return, and now there was major trouble at Sugar Works. Aside from Chase and her family, the birch syrup company had been her life's work. She would do anything she could to make sure things didn't fall apart on her watch.

When Violet walked into the inn, she quickly noticed the front desk was empty. Where was Sadie? Now that her aunt and uncle were older, Sadie had taken over the reins of the establishment, and she could usually be found manning the welcome desk.

She followed the low hum of voices toward the dining area, where she spotted Deacon sitting at a table by himself. Sadie was pouring him coffee from a large carafe and chatting with Deacon. Violet found herself tongue-tied for a moment as she approached the table. Seeing Deacon still caused butterflies to flutter around in her belly. His hair looked slightly damp, as if he'd just taken a shower. The ends were a bit wavy. Overall, the years had been very kind to him. He was an extremely handsome man who was very fit, someone who clearly maintained an active lifestyle.

Had he left a partner back in Seattle? Surely he hadn't been single all this time, yet the thought of him being involved with a romantic partner caused a little hitch in her heart. She was being ridiculous. Their relationship was a thing of the past.

"Violet! Long time no see!" Sadie said, reaching out to hug her.

"Sadie, you look amazing. Motherhood suits you," Violet said.

"Thank you. Speaking of which, I need to check that she's still napping," she said with a laugh before rushing off.

Deacon looked surprised as he stood to greet her. *Lord, please let him be receptive to helping out at Sugar Works. We need all the hands we can get at the moment.*

"Violet. What are you doing here? Is everything okay with Chase?" he asked. His height and broad shoulders never failed to make an impression on her. In dark-wash jeans and a plaid shirt, he looked relaxed and comfortable in his surroundings.

She motioned for him to sit down. "Please, don't stand up on my account. I wanted to ask you something, and I didn't want to do it over the phone. Sorry to interrupt your meal," she apologized. A part of her wanted to turn right around and leave. Why did things feel so awkward between them? In many ways, it seemed as if they were starting from scratch in their relationship.

"Okay, shoot," he said, pushing his plate away. "And please take a seat. Would you like some coffee?"

"No thanks," she said, letting out a nervous laugh. "If I have any more, I'll be bouncing off the walls." She sat down and drummed her fingers on the table. "I know you said that you're sticking around town for a bit. Is that still the case?"

Deacon nodded his head. "One hundred percent. After that talk with Chase, I'm more determined than ever to bond with him. I can't do that from Chicago. It's important that I'm hands-on with him and we're making memories." His jaw tightened. "I hope you're not here to tell me to pace myself."

"No, Deacon. This actually isn't about Chase. It's about Sugar Works."

Deacon frowned. "What's going on?"

"We have a situation with diseased trees on the property while at the same time a number of our employees have been slammed by a stomach virus. When it rains, it pours." A sigh slipped past her lips. There was a lot resting on her shoulders.

"I'm sorry to hear that. I know that must be stressful." Sympathy radiated from Deacon's voice. She knew that he understood based on his experience working with trees. He had helped with this very same issue when he'd previously worked at Sugar Works. According to what he'd once told her, his family was involved in landscaping.

"It is worrisome, mostly for my dad. Which is why I'm here." She locked gazes with him. "We were wondering if you would consider coming to work for us. Since you're going to be living here for a bit and you have experience with the company..." She was babbling now, unnerved by his steady gaze, but she pressed on. "We figured you might be open to working with us, even if it's just until this crisis is over." She fiddled with her fingers. "Unless of course you've accepted a job elsewhere." He had only been in town for a few days, but it was possible Deacon had found another position. It wouldn't be the end of the world, but Abel would be disappointed. And if she was being honest, Chase wanted Deacon around more often.

"Of course I would be open to it," he answered. "I loved being a part of the Sugar Works family. It gave me a sense of purpose I'd never experienced before. Or since."

His comment hung in the air, reminding Violet of all that once was. He had been like a member of the Drummond family, trusted and beloved by all of them. She felt a squeezing sensation in her chest as the memories came crashing to the surface. All of her hopes and dreams had been tied up in this man she had loved beyond measure. Letting go of those feelings hadn't been easy, but she'd done it and built a new life for herself, only to have Deacon return to disrupt her orderly life.

She wasn't sure if she would ever truly get past what had happened.

And now, against her better judgment, they would be working together. She knew what it was like to work side by side with him for a common purpose. It was how they had fallen in love all those years ago. A ripple of fear passed through her.

Was her heart vulnerable to Deacon? On some level, was that the reason she'd been hesitant to have him come on board?

"So when do I start?" Deacon asked, leaning across the table eagerly. His expression was so hopeful and endearing, serving as a reminder that he was still the person she'd once known.

"Yesterday," she said, mustering a smile. Deacon's exuberance was reassuring.

"All right then," Deacon said, jumping to his feet. "Let me put some things in a backpack, and I'll meet you out front."

"Sure thing," she said, walking toward the lobby. Sadie was standing by the front desk, cradling her baby in her arms.

"What a sweetheart," Violet cooed as she looked down at the darling baby swaddled in a blanket. "She's growing more beautiful by the day."

"Thank you. She's a handful some days,

but a blessing every day," Sadie said, jiggling her baby girl. "How are things going with… Deacon?" Sadie asked, raising an eyebrow.

"So far so good, I suppose. He's going to be helping out at Sugar Works, and of course he plans to get to know Chase." She shrugged, unsure of what else to say. "It's been quite a shock to the system to say the least."

"I can only imagine," Sadie answered, making a tutting sound. "I'm still having a hard time with the new name. It must be really difficult for you."

"Honestly, I know Deacon's been through a lot, not to mention he's lost so much time with Chase. That makes it hard to host a pity party for myself." She was speaking from the heart and being completely honest. The situation was difficult, but she couldn't even imagine the depth of Deacon's struggles. Even though she wanted him to take things slowly with Chase, she knew that he was trying to make up for lost time. Who could blame him?

"You're a compassionate person, Violet, but it's okay to acknowledge the toll this has taken on you as well," Sadie told her.

"Thanks, my friend," she said, feeling grateful that her feelings were being considered. Serenity Peak was a wonderful place, but it could also be prone to gossip. So many of the townsfolk would be swept up in the drama of Deacon's return that she would be a mere afterthought, along with Chase. Yes, the situation was shocking, but it was also rife with potential pitfalls. At this moment, all she could do was move forward with grace and do her best to facilitate a healthy relationship between him and their son.

Violet wouldn't hesitate to step in if things got too intense for Chase or if she felt Deacon was pushing too hard and too fast. For his entire life, Chase had only experienced one parental influence. She worried that things might get complicated moving forward.

Chase was and would always be the most important person in her life. She would do whatever was necessary to protect him.

Chapter Six

Deacon followed behind Violet's truck as she led the way to Sugar Works. She was driving to the area of the property where the diseased trees were located. Deacon knew that there was a distinct possibility that other trees had been affected. Although this area had been identified, he knew from past experience that birch borers could cut a large swath through birch trees. It could happen swiftly, without anyone being aware it was happening until it was too late. Violet knew this as well, and he sensed she was worried about this possibility.

Abel was there with a few of his workers, surveying the area. When he saw Deacon, he came striding over. "Thanks so much for agreeing to come back to work here," Abel said, reaching out and clapping Deacon heartily on the shoulder. "We are truly grateful. I'm familiar with the borer issue, but I can't be everywhere at once."

"Thanks for welcoming me back," Deacon said, moved by Abel's gratitude. He had always looked up to Abel as a wonderful father and a man of faith. There had never been a negative word exchanged between them. If things had been different, Deacon would have loved for this man to be his father-in-law. Moving forward, he would settle for Abel being his boss and a trusted friend. He wanted Abel, as Chase's grandfather, to think well of him. It was his pleasure to lend a hand at Sugar Works. He well understood that as the head of the company, Abel had a lot of fires to put out. He couldn't work exclusively in this one area while he also had to oversee the production of the birch syrup.

"We've started the process of treating this batch of trees, but unfortunately, it's too late to save a portion of them," Abel said, his brows knit together.

"I'm wondering if we took too long to notice the problem," Violet said, chewing her lip. It was something she'd always done when she was worried about something. Clearly that hadn't changed.

"Try to think positive, Vi," he said, his nickname for her just slipping out.

Deacon went over and examined some of the nearby trees. It was evident at first glance that they were infected from the wilting and dying off of their upper crowns. Violet had moved to stand beside him, and she too was looking closely at the trees.

"These ridges and holes in the bark are indicative of disease," he said, running his fingers along the tree. "It seems pretty extensive past the area being treated."

She let out a little groan. "That's what we suspected. Clyde Brown was out here examining the trees for us, but he's taken ill like a lot of other workers."

"It's unfortunate that two calamities are happening at the same time," Deacon said.

"We're trying to get some temporary staff to fill in," Violet explained. "But a lot of our existing employees are still learning about birch syrup production, so they're not necessarily adept at dealing with this particular issue."

"I think we need to check every section of birch trees. This can spread quickly." He didn't want to say it out loud, but he had a sinking sensation in the pit of his stomach. Sugar Works could lose a lot of birch trees, which was always heartbreaking and could be financially devastating.

Violet bit her lip. "We have people looking in other sections as we speak, but honestly, it takes a trained eye to identify the damage."

He also knew that to be true. A cursory inspection could miss signs of disease at its earliest stages. Given the large property, it would take a massive amount of hours and work to properly inspect all of the trees. Thankfully, his father had taught him at an early age how to recognize this sort of infestation.

"Well, the good news is that you've already identified the problem and you're treating the trees. We can all pray to salvage as many trees as possible," he told her.

Deacon looked out over the swath of trees. The mountains were visible in the background, stunning and awe-inspiring. God's masterpiece. They served as a reminder that He had created all of the beauty surrounding them. Ultimately only He could see Sugar Works through this crisis. They just had to believe.

"I've been all over this country, and as

of yet, there's nothing that compares to this amazing vista. It's breathtaking." He let out a sigh of appreciation, grateful to be standing here.

Violet nodded. "There's something so grounding about this land. It's timeless. One hundred years from now, it's still going to look the same," Violet said, gazing off into the distance. "It will still matter."

He tried not to stare, but her profile showed grace and strength. As a single mother, she'd needed both. Once again, guilt pierced his insides. What he would give to turn back the clock. He would have risked the danger to himself for Chase and Violet.

"It makes me happy thinking of our son being raised in such a magnificent setting." That knowledge settled over him like a warm blanket. Even though he hadn't been around to help raise him, Deacon was reassured by the idea of Chase growing up in this place, getting to explore every inch of this rugged land. With the wind in his hair and snow falling all around him, Deacon imagined. Sheer heaven for a kid.

"Chase loves living here in Serenity Peak. His life would be pretty perfect if he could have a dog," she said, chuckling lightly.

"Can't blame him for that. I loved growing up with a dog," Deacon told her. "Labrador retrievers. Huskies. Beautiful dogs."

"Me too. I just don't have the time right now to train a dog," Violet said, looking regretful. "But sooner or later, it's going to happen. He just has to be patient."

"I missed this place," Deacon said, breathing in the pristine air. "It always felt like home to me." Of course, he had missed his family back in Chicago, but this place had given him refuge and a sense of belonging. To this day, no place had nestled into his heart in the same way.

Violet met his gaze for a moment then looked away. "I never imagined you would leave like that. You were so at home here."

"I used to pray every night that I wouldn't have to, but then I messed up by calling home," he told her. "Living in Serenity Peak was a haven for me. I felt like I was a part of the fabric of this town, and it broke my heart to walk away from it all." *And you*, he wanted to say. *Especially you.*

"Well, that was all in the past," she said crisply. "It's best for all of us to keep ourselves grounded in the present." He thought he saw a sheen of tears in her eyes, but she quickly blinked them away. Deacon sensed that talking about their shared past wasn't easy for her. At some point down the road, perhaps she would open up to him and tell him what she'd been through. He was convinced that Violet had a story to tell, one she didn't share with many people.

"Deacon!" He whirled around at the sound of a child's voice calling out to him and spotted a school bus heading down the road. Chase was running toward him at breakneck speed, a smile lighting up his face. When Chase reached him, Deacon held his arms out. His son's movements were a bit tentative, so Deacon let go after a few moments, not wanting to overwhelm him. How strange it was that a few days ago he hadn't even known about his son. Now, a whole new world was opening up. The dark days had receded, and he was standing here full of hope and the promise of new beginnings.

God was good!

"Are you helping out with the trees?" Chase asked. "Mom said some of them were dying." Chase's expression was full of concern. Being raised around Sugar Works had given Chase knowledge of what such devastation could mean.

"Yep. I'm working for Sugar Works now with your mom and granddad," Deacon said, his chest puffing out a little bit at the look of joy radiating from his son. He hadn't had much to be proud of in a long time. Working for Abel Drummond, who was solid and honorable, made him feel good about himself. Not having to hide his true identity or keep a low profile at all times was a liberating feeling.

"That's so cool," Chase said, pumping his fist in the air. "It's like we're all on the same team."

Violet and Deacon both chuckled. "That's a good way to look at it," Violet said, looking down at Chase as if he'd hung the moon. Love was evident in every single interaction Violet had with Chase. Although Deacon felt a strong pull in his son's direction, he knew their bond was still a work in progress. He longed for the day when they could share an amazing rapport and finish each other's sentences. He wanted Chase to call him Dad, but he knew it was far too soon for such a step. If he pushed in any way, it could backfire on him, not just with Chase but with Violet as well.

"Can I hang out with you guys for a bit?" Chase asked, crossing his hands prayerfully in front of him.

"What about homework?" Violet asked, making a face. "You need to keep those grades up."

"It's pretty light tonight," Chase said. "Please, please, please."

Violet glanced over at Deacon. He nodded at her, letting her know it was all right with him. Spending time with Chase was high on his priority list.

"Okay, but only for a short while. Then you have to scoot," Violet said, earning herself a grateful hug from Chase.

"Let's take a ride out to another area so we can check more trees," Deacon suggested. That way they would have a better idea of the overall damage.

"Good idea, since I don't think Clyde got very far before taking ill. Let's take my truck," Violet said, motioning toward the two of them.

As Deacon began to follow behind her in lockstep with Chase, he felt his son's hand in his. Chase was holding on tightly as if he didn't want to let go. Deacon looked down at the sight of their linked hands. He could feel a smile twitching at the corners of his lips. This, he thought, was one of life's simple pleasures, the likes of which he'd never known. A son! He actually had a son.

When he'd called home and told his father about Chase, Ben Shaw had cried at the news and told him how proud his mother would have been. A part of him ached to think about his mother being gone and the fact that she wouldn't ever get to be a grandmother to Chase. At moments like this, he struggled against giving in to bitterness and anger. Since becoming a man of faith, he'd learned to lean in to prayer rather than rage against the unfairness of life.

"Shotgun!" Chase called out as he ran toward the truck. With a deep-throated laugh, Deacon raced him, beating his son by mere seconds.

"Hey!" Chase complained. "Aren't you supposed to let me win?"

"Absolutely not," Deacon said. "That would be a hollow victory, son. In the long run, it wouldn't mean anything."

"Yeah it would. To me," Chase said, a befuddled look on his face.

Deacon laughed as he vaulted into the front seat of Violet's truck. Chase was about to learn a thing or two about his dear old dad. Deacon didn't believe in faking victories. Working hard to get better at something shaped character, even if it was as inconsequential as a foot race.

Chase was glaring at him. "Mom always lets me win. You should too." Suddenly, his lip was stuck out, and he was pouting.

"Well, the last time I looked, I'm not her," Deacon shot back. He didn't like the edge in Chase's voice. And the boy needed to know he couldn't manipulate Deacon.

Deacon couldn't quite make out Chase's muttered response, but he had the feeling that it wasn't anything good. For a second, Deacon wondered if he was in over his head. Moments ago, Chase had been jovial, but he'd turned on a dime. He was sitting in the back of the truck with his arms folded across his chest. The light-hearted mood had quickly evaporated.

"Mom, just let me out at the house. I want to go home," Chase grumbled.

Deacon opened his mouth, then closed it. Should he try to convince Chase to change his mind and accompany them? Or should he just leave it alone and let him stew?

Violet looked over at him as she revved the truck's engine. "Welcome to parent-hood," Violet said, a little sigh passing her lips. "Expect the unexpected."

Well, no one had ever said parenthood

was easy. He literally had zero experience with kids, and he had no clue how to handle Chase's petulant mood. He imagined giving in would be the easiest solution, but he wasn't about to cater to a nine-year-old's temper tantrum. Nor was he going to encourage him to act out when he didn't get his way on something. Later, when they were alone, he planned to ask Violet about her parenting style so they could find the best way to co-parent.

Deacon's mind wandered as he gazed out the window at the lush Alaskan scenery. He sucked in the fresh air, all the while reminding himself that his appearance in his son's life had been out of the blue and a bit chaotic. Chase had barely had time to process the fact that his father had turned up in Serenity Peak after a lifetime of not knowing him.

Maybe Violet had been right. Perhaps this was all moving too quickly for Chase. His heart sank at the prospect of taking a step back from getting to know his son, but he had to tread carefully with him or run the risk of the entire situation falling apart.

Violet's heart sank as she watched Chase jump out of the back of the truck and march toward the house. His body language spoke volumes. He was upset and frustrated. And it was all her fault. She'd known that meeting his father so abruptly would put him into a tailspin. It was understandable after all. Violet had spent the last nine years avoiding the truth, and she'd allowed her own hurts to get in the way of being straightforward and honest.

Not that she should make excuses for Chase. His behavior had been bratty and rude. She didn't want Deacon to think poorly of their son.

"What did I do wrong?" Deacon asked. "Things were going so well. He was even holding my hand."

Her heart went out to him. She touched

his arm, trying to reassure him. "You didn't do anything wrong. This isn't about losing a race to the truck or you not letting him win. It's about him struggling with suddenly having a father. Everything about you is new to him."

"So what exactly did you tell him about me?"

Violet looked away from him. She was feeling pretty guilty at the moment. She answered in a low voice. "I did tell him that you left town before I found out I was pregnant."

"And that's it? Nothing at all about our relationship or that I worked for your family's company?" Deacon asked, his tone radiating pain.

"No, I'm sorry. I just didn't think it was in his best interest to hear about a man I thought chose to walk away from me." She felt really small admitting it, but this was her truth.

"No wonder Chase is confused. You erased me from the equation, thoroughly and completely. I wasn't even a footnote in my son's life." His mouth was set in a hard line.

He had never been quick to anger, but there was no denying it. Deacon was livid.

"What do you think I should have told him? That we were engaged and in love then you left me without a backward glance? I didn't want to weigh him down with all those things." Her lips trembled uncontrollably.

He looked out the window rather than in her direction. "It just seems harsh that he didn't know a single thing of substance about me."

That was fair. If she had to go back in time, she would do things differently. She'd had no right to withhold that sort of information from their son.

"I didn't want him to think that you'd abandoned him. That you didn't want him. That kind of information can wreck a kid. So I made sure to tell him that you didn't know I was pregnant." She tightly gripped the steering wheel. "It's not fair of you to judge me. You were the one who left. I understand why now, but I didn't have a clue then. I was left to my own devices, so I did the best I knew how."

He bowed his head, and the silence stretched out between them with neither one saying a word. By the time Violet arrived at the northern part of the property, the vehicle was filled with tension. When she parked and turned the ignition off, Deacon placed his hand on her arm. Even though she had a coat on, her body reacted immediately to the contact, with warmth spreading along her arm.

"I'm sorry," Deacon said. "Of course none of this is your fault. You did what you thought was best, and I imagine it was." He turned to look at her. "It just hurts knowing I wasn't even a glimmer in his eye all of this time. I would give anything in this world to have been a part of his life. They say God never gives you more than you can handle, but honestly, it feels like it's all been piling up on me over the years." He let out a groan. "I can't seem to catch a break."

Honestly, she couldn't imagine going through what he had endured—loss, alienation, fear. But she truly believed that better days were in store for him. He had been given a fresh lease on life.

"You've been through it, Deacon, that's for sure, but this little hiccup with Chase is nothing compared to all the other things you've endured. It will all blow over."

"You really think so?" he asked, turning toward her.

"I know so. This too shall pass. Like you told me earlier, think positive." She flashed him a wide smile.

"Thanks for lifting me up," Deacon said. "That's always been a special skill of yours."

"Of course," she said, feeling her chest flutter at the praise.

As they looked at one another something hummed and pulsed in the air between them. It startled Violet so much she was almost afraid to breathe. He was sitting so close to her that she could smell the aroma of his woodsy aftershave. She could hear the sound of his light breathing. Violet had almost forgotten about the small scar above his right eye, a remnant of a skateboarding accident as a child. Barely visible freckles dotted the bridge of his nose.

"Violet, I—" he began, before a knock on the truck's driver-side window interrupted him.

Violet turned toward the sound, appreciating the slight reprieve from whatever Deacon had been about to say to her. She couldn't be certain, but she'd sensed it had been something that would make her emotional. She didn't need or want to go on a trip with him down memory lane. Deacon was a dangerous person because he was the only man she'd ever loved. He brought out feelings in her that made her incredibly vulnerable. These days, she needed her strength.

She rolled down her window at the sight of Horace Sharpe, one of their workers. Dedicated and hardworking, Horace had been with Sugar Works since the beginning.

"Hey, Horace. What's going on?" she asked, trying to ignore the defeated expression on his face. Normally upbeat, his body language spoke volumes.

"Violet," he said with a nod. "We've been going through this area, and I'm fairly certain that the birch trees in this section are dying."

Chapter Seven

Deacon hated hearing the news about the additional section of diseased trees, but he loved seeing Violet take control of the situation. Over the past ten years, she had grown into her position as Abel's second-in-command and it showed. She was professional and calm in the way she interacted with her employees. The workers clearly respected and liked her. She put him to work right away, and Deacon couldn't remember ever feeling so invigorated. By the time they called it a day, the sky had turned a navy blue, and a pale sliver of moon was visible along with a smattering of stars.

Abel had headed over to the house earlier to make Chase dinner and check his homework. His presence in his grandson's life demonstrated the importance of family connections. Deacon longed for the day he could introduce his own family to Chase. He could take him to Wrigley Field for a baseball game and order him a deep dish pizza at his favorite joint. Now that he knew about Chase, he was stuck in an impossible position. His aging father was waiting for him back in Chicago, yet he'd missed nine years of Chase's life. Both worlds were tugging at his heart. Whatever road he didn't take would make his soul ache.

"Thanks for being here," Violet told him as the crew began to disperse. "You're a great asset to Sugar Works."

"Happy to help out," Deacon said. "I'll be back in the morning, first thing." There was still a lot of work to be done to recover from the birch tree crisis. He would stay on board for as long as they wanted and needed him. Work always gave him a sense of validation, especially when he was doing something he loved. There was nothing better than banding together as a team to solve problems.

On the way back to the Forget-Me-Not Inn, Deacon's mind wandered. He needed to spend time with Chase and strengthen their relationship. He wanted to learn all the ins and outs of being a father. Tomorrow was a new day, and he was hoping that they could work through this rough patch. Violet knew Chase better than anyone, and she'd been convinced that it would blow over.

Deacon didn't really know much about Chase. What was his favorite color? Who was his best friend? Was he into pizza or burgers? Was he a good student or average, as Deacon himself had been?

Dogs. He knew that Chase loved dogs. Matter of fact, he dreamed of having one of his own. Gideon had told him about a woman in town, Destiny, who trained service dogs on her property. Maybe they could visit the property and meet the dogs. He vaguely remembered her older brother, Charlie. Excitement flared inside of him at the idea of presenting Chase with a fun outing.

On his way back to the inn, Deacon made a last-minute decision to stop by Northern Lights for a takeout order. He was exhausted from a long day's work, but he was hungry. Deacon also wanted to get some information from Sean if he was around. Once he stepped inside, he quickly spotted Sean serving customers big plates overflowing with seafood.

Once he was done with his customers, Sean warmly greeted him, handing him a menu after he inquired about ordering something to go.

"Let me know what you want to order," Sean said, stepping behind the counter. "We have some great salmon tonight."

"Sounds good to me," Deacon said. He was so hungry just about anything sounded good. He had never once been disappointed with the food at Northern Lights, so he wasn't worried.

"Coming right up," Sean said. "Why don't you take a seat. It'll be a few minutes."

Deacon sat down at one of the counter seats as Sean popped open a can of soda and placed the drink in front of him. "Thanks," he said with a nod. "Hey, can you give me more info on the dog trainer you were telling me about? Destiny, right?"

"Sure thing. She's Charlie's little sister. Destiny Johnson. Really sweet and knows her way around dogs." Sean frowned. "Are you looking for a service dog?"

"No," Deacon said, taking a swig of his soda. "But Chase loves dogs, and I need to make some inroads with him. I thought Destiny might let us visit her place and play with the dogs. Maybe give us a tour in exchange for a donation to her program."

"I don't see why she wouldn't," Sean said, taking out his phone. "I'll forward you her contact information."

"Thanks," Deacon said, hearing the ping on his phone from Sean's text.

Sean leaned over the counter and began speaking in a low tone. "So, how are things with you and Violet? Any lingering feelings?"

Feelings? He hadn't stopped to examine how he felt, but he knew that she still meant the world to him.

"I have wonderful memories of the time we had together," he admitted. "I wanted to spend the rest of my life with Violet. She'll always be special to me." Just saying the words out loud caused a little pang in his heart. It was hard stuffing down all the recollections of their relationship and the plans they'd made for a future together.

"So all that is over and done with?"

Sean asked. "I'm only asking because I remember the two of you falling in love. You guys were the real deal."

He had thought the same thing. Everything had fallen apart because of his past and being in witness protection. The reality of it made him want to scream out loud.

He let out a ragged sigh. "Sean, there's a huge divide between us, and it seems almost impossible to cross it."

"I get it," Sean said. "Ten years is a long time to be apart."

"Which is why I'm focusing on Chase. Honestly, she's been through so much, more than I know, most likely. And it's all because of me."

"Autumn!" Sean called out as a striking woman walked in the back door. She had a baby perched on her hip. Autumn was Sean's younger sister, and according to Sadie, she was now married to Judah Campbell, a local fisherman. A journalist by trade, Autumn had always been a no-nonsense woman with a big heart.

She made her way over, a big smile lighting up her face. He couldn't help but notice her grin fading as soon as she spotted him. Although he hadn't known Autumn for long, she had always been friendly. Until now.

Sean began cooing at his nephew and lifted him into his arms.

"Let me go check on your food with River," Sean said, nervously looking back and forth between them before going in the back with the baby.

"Hey, Autumn," he said. "How's it going?"

She nodded at him. "Hello there. I guess that I can't call you John anymore," she said, a hard edge to her tone.

"I prefer Deacon," he told her. "It's my given name."

"So Sean told me," she said, clearing her throat. "I'm sorry for what you've been through. It sounds awful."

"It was, but it's all over now, which is a blessing. I can build a relationship with my son, so I consider myself blessed."

She nodded. "You deserve a fresh start, but my concern is that you're going to hurt not only Chase but Violet as well. She's my best friend in the world, and I can't bear to see her life get torn apart again."

Yikes. He hadn't imagined that Autumn would call him out, although he knew that she and Violet had been besties since their teen years. She was protective of Violet, which he understood. He wasn't the only one who had gone through extremely difficult times. He'd left heartache in his wake.

"I—I don't intend to hurt anyone. The reason I came back was in order to make amends," he told her. "That's part of my fresh start. And I'm happy that I took that leap of faith because if I hadn't, I would never have found out about Chase. And that knowledge has changed my world."

Just then Sean returned with a bag that he held out to Deacon. "Is everything good here?" he asked, darting a nervous glance at his sister.

"We're fine, Sean," Autumn said. "Just getting a few things straight."

Deacon took his food then said his goodbyes and headed out to the parking lot. He settled in the driver's seat and revved the engine. Although Autumn was a nice person, their run-in had been a bit awkward. Coming back to Serenity Peak made him feel at times as if he was walking a tightrope. Some folks were understanding about him being in the WIT-SEC program, while others didn't seem to trust him. It hurt way more than he wanted to acknowledge. He had been a victim of circumstance, but some folks disregarded that, choosing instead to see him in a negative light.

Even though he was no longer in witness protection and he was free to live his life without the threat of danger, there were still obstacles standing in his way.

At moments like this one, it seemed as if he was fighting an uphill battle simply to exist in Serenity Peak.

There was nothing Violet liked better than a lazy Saturday morning with nothing on her agenda other than sleeping in, sitting in her reading nook with a favorite book and hanging out with Chase. With the current situation with the diseased birch trees, today was shaping up to be another work day. At her father's insistence, they were taking the morning off, since resting their bodies was important in order to replenish themselves.

"Nothing will be gained by overextending ourselves," Abel had said. "It might be a perfect time to break bread with Autumn and Judah," he'd suggested. "Why don't you invite them over?"

"That's a great idea," Violet said. "I

haven't seen Autumn in a bit. I'll give Skye a call as well."

"Violet, I think it might be the right thing for us to invite Deacon as well. He's really been a godsend in our time of need."

Deacon. Her pulse began to race at the thought of him being in such an intimate gathering with her. It was getting harder and harder to simply view him as Chase's father without allowing memories of their relationship to creep in. But her dad was right. It would be the kind thing to do. Deacon was all alone in Serenity Peak, with the exception of a few old friends who had families of their own.

"You're right," she said. "He's been so helpful. I don't mind if you give him a call."

A short while later, she let Chase know about his dad being invited over for brunch. Her son regarded her with wide eyes and an open mouth, no doubt recalling his behavior from the other day. He would have to find a way to make things right with Deacon on his own. He was almost ten years old, and Violet was beginning to realize that she couldn't do everything for him.

Autumn and Judah showed up with pastries, a fruit platter and banana bread for their brunch. Violet had whipped up two large quiches, hash browns and sausages, while Skye made cinnamon rolls and latkes.

Deacon hadn't arrived yet, but everyone else had shown up. Both Skye and Autumn were helping her in the kitchen with food prep. Autumn's husband, Judah, was outside with Abel, Chase and Ryan while baby River was napping. Skye's daughter, Lula, was in a high chair, happily eating a snack.

Autumn put a hand on her hip and faced Violet. "So, why haven't you reached out to me, Violet? I had to find out about John's return from Sean."

"You mean Deacon, not John," Violet

corrected. "And my dad invited him to brunch so don't talk so loud."

Autumn slapped her hand to her forehead and let out a giggle. "It's not funny, but I feel like we're in an episode of *Law & Order*. Witness protection? Changed names?"

"What's that saying?" Skye asked. "Truth is stranger than fiction."

"It sure is," Violet said, shaking her head. "It all feels pretty surreal. But it's all true, and he's been through a lot."

"How are things with Chase?" Autumn asked as she sliced her banana bread. "Is everything good on that front?"

Both Autumn and Skye were looking at her, awaiting a response.

Violet shrugged lightly. "A mixed bag. He's really excited to have a dad in his life, and Deacon is determined to create a bond, so I'm fairly optimistic. As long as they take it slow and not rush things. Chase has a tendency to get overwhelmed."

"That makes sense," Skye said. "This is a huge change for him."

She was still worried about how Chase was processing having an instant father on his hands. If only she had told him more about Deacon, something that would have given him a foundation for their relationship. If she could go back in time, she would do things differently. But she wasn't going to beat herself up about it. Never in a million years had she imagined that Deacon would walk back into their lives—and with a really good reason for having left. And now she was worried about him leaving Chase in the lurch.

"I think all the food is heated up," Skye said as she took one of the quiches out of the oven. "Let's eat."

"I'll go gather everybody from outside," Autumn said before heading toward the back door.

"Violet." Deacon was standing in the entryway of the kitchen. He was holding out a bouquet of forget-me-nots. "I didn't want to come empty-handed."

Violet took the vibrant floral arrangement from Deacon, her fingers brushing against his in the process. She felt a little jolt at the contact. "Thank you," she said. "You're just in time for brunch." She waved him toward the dining room, trailing after him, her pulse racing wildly. Her father stood up from the table and offered Deacon the seat next to him, with Chase on the other side.

As she sat down at the table, her mind was filled with one single thought.

Despite the lost years between them, she wasn't indifferent to Deacon. Not by a long shot.

Being at the Drummonds' house wasn't nearly as uncomfortable as he'd imagined. From the moment he had walked through the doors, everyone treated him like an honored guest. And no one peppered him with questions about the Witness Protection Program, which was nice. He was able to be a part of the gathering without feeling on the spot. He was getting pretty tired of telling his story over and over again.

After brunch was over, Chase tugged on his shirt sleeve and pulled him to the side to talk to him.

"I'm sorry about the other day," Chase said in a low voice as he shifted from one foot to the other. He seemed embarrassed. He wasn't looking him in the eye during his apology. "I don't know why I got so upset, but I was rude. And you didn't deserve that."

"Chase, it takes a lot of courage to apologize." He placed a hand over his heart. "I really appreciate it. You're a fine young man. We all have our moments. As long as we learn from them then we become better people in the long run."

Chase grinned at him. "I sure did learn a lesson. That's a promise."

Deacon knew that most likely there

would be other moments where Chase acted up. He was a kid after all, and nine-year-olds were far from perfect. He accepted that there would be ups and downs. He just needed to embrace him, flaws and all.

He had a surprise up his sleeve. Deacon had reached out to Destiny, who had graciously invited them to visit her property and check out the dog training program.

"I have something to ask you," Deacon said. "How would you like to visit a place in town that trains service dogs? It'll give you a chance to play with some canines."

Chase let out a howl. "Are you serious? Of course I want to go. I love dogs." He reached out and placed his arm around him in a sweet gesture. Within seconds, he was racing off to tell Abel the news.

Deacon grinned at the exuberance Chase displayed. It felt good that he'd made his son so happy. All of a sudden, he felt as if he could leap buildings in a single bound.

Violet walked over, a look of curiosity etched on her face. "What was that all about? He looks as if he just won a ticket to the moon."

"Nothing as exciting as a trip to the moon, but I did invite him to a service-dog training farm in the area," Deacon explained, a smile twitching at his lips.

Violet let out a surprised sound. Immediately he wondered if he should have asked her first. They had never set any ground rules for him spending time with Chase. Had he messed up?

"Destiny's place, I assume? She's doing great work out there and helping out a lot of folks who need service dogs. She's in high demand in Serenity Peak."

"I'm sorry for not running this by you before I mentioned it to Chase." He made a face. "I suppose that I was just so excited about finding common ground with our son that I let it slip."

"Oh, it's not a problem. Despite what I said about wanting you to pace yourself with Chase, I really do want you in his life. He deserves a father."

Warmth spread through his chest at the kind sentiments she'd expressed. Ever since finding out that Chase was his son, Deacon had been doubting himself and his ability to truly be a father. But with Violet cheering him on, he suddenly felt worthy of the job.

"That means a lot to me. I have a lot to learn about being a dad, but I'm willing to do whatever it takes." He let out a chuckle. "I just found out over brunch that Chase loves banana bread. I think he devoured three slices."

Violet laughed along with him. "It might have been four. He's going through a growth spurt."

"Excuse me," Abel said as he approached them. "I'm going to switch up my clothes and head out." He looked at Deacon. "Thanks for joining us for brunch. It's nice to see you and Chase bonding." He placed a hand on Deacon's shoulder.

"I appreciate you including me," Deacon said. "It means a lot to me."

"I'll join you shortly, Daddy," Violet said. "I need to put my work clothes on as well."

Abel walked off with a wave. His stride was powerful and full of purpose.

"I can work today if you need me, Violet," Deacon offered. "I'd like to spend some time with Chase since I'm here, but I can head out and join you in a bit."

A smile lit up her face. "I sincerely appreciate the offer. We're still putting out fires, so to speak." She ran a hand through her long hair, brushing it out of her face. He had always loved the fiery color. In certain lights, it glowed like the sun. "I can't wait until things are back to normal around here."

Normal? He hadn't experienced any normalcy in over a decade. Being on the run had taken a huge toll on him, both physically and emotionally. But being back in Serenity Peak made him think it might just be possible. He couldn't help but wonder if that was wise. Getting too settled might give him a false sense of security. In his experience, that was when you had the rug pulled out from underneath you.

Deacon had come back to Alaska to make amends with Violet, but once he had discovered he was a father, his goals had shifted. Now he found himself being pulled back into Violet's orbit. And he wasn't sure that, after all this time, he even fit into her world.

Chapter Eight

For the next week, Deacon worked side by side with Abel, Violet and the rest of the Sugar Works employees. Long days stretched into evenings as they tackled the crisis at hand. According to Abel, the worst of the infestation was over. Seeing the relief on the older man's face was heartwarming. Being a part of the Sugar Works crew made him feel as if he was part of something wonderful. Accepted and appreciated. Those things had been hard to come by during his years on the run.

During his years in Maine and Seattle,

he had forged friendships, but he had always been on guard and unable to completely lean in to those relationships. In some ways, he'd never managed to move past the life he had led in Serenity Peak.

At the moment, he, Violet and the team were doing another sweep of the birch trees after having treated the ones that were salvageable. Seeing so much destruction was weighing heavily on all of them. All of a sudden, a crackling sound filled the air. Acting on pure instinct, Deacon reached for Violet and pulled her behind a copse of trees.

"Stay down!" he shouted as he shielded her with his body. He was breathing heavily, and a sheen of moisture pooled on his forehead.

"Deacon. What are you doing?" Violet asked, her eyes wide. "Nothing's wrong. It was just one of the trucks backfiring."

A vehicle backfiring? He wiped his brow with the back of his hand. He had thought for a few terrifying moments that someone was trying to harm them. To his ears, it had sounded like gunshots. His mouth felt as if it was filled with cotton, and his pulse raced wildly.

"I'm sorry. I need a few minutes to get myself together," he said, the words spilling out. "I'll be right back."

He strode away from Violet, his mind spinning over what just happened. He'd acted as if he was still in the Witness Protection Program. After so many years on the run, it was extremely difficult to put the fear behind him. Although he knew on a rational level that the danger had passed with the deaths of Gus Salomon, the head of the Chicago-based crime family, and his criminal cohorts, a part of him was still stuck in limbo. He wanted true freedom. And that meant no longer living in dread and fear. Here he was, in a tranquil small town in Alaska, yet still trapped by panic and anxiety.

Lord, please give me a spirit of faith

*and not fear. I'm so tired of living my life
in the shadows.*

A few minutes later, he headed back
to where he'd left Violet. She was gazing at him with a look of concern, her
brows knit together. "Deacon, what just
happened? Are you all right?" she asked.
"Talk to me."

He shook his head, embarrassment taking hold of him. How could he explain it
in a way that Violet would understand?
Sometimes he didn't even understand
why he couldn't move past the panic he
felt when there were loud, sudden noises
or a stranger walking behind him. He
wished that he could just lean into the
fact that he was finally free of WITSEC.
But that didn't mean he wasn't still men-
tally imprisoned.

"I thought we were in danger," he said.
"Old habits die hard, I suppose. For so
many years, I was on the run, hiding
from people who wanted to hurt me.
There were many times when the dan-

ger got really close, and I had to be fast on my feet to avoid being killed. I've had shots taken at me before. I've literally run for my life. Even here—before I left Serenity Peak, someone tried to run me off the road. Remember the man with the weapon who was taken into custody at Sugar Works? I fully believe he was sent by the Salomon family." He shuddered. "Every now and again, something happens that brings me back to that terrible time. I guess that I still have a lot of work to do on myself."

Violet quirked her mouth. "Oh, Deacon. I'm so sorry. You've been through such an ordeal."

"No, I'm sorry," he said. "I don't ever want you to question whether Chase is in danger, because he isn't. The Salomon family is no longer a threat. It's just not as easy as I thought it would be to put it all behind me."

"That's understandable. You spent the last decade in the Witness Protection

Program, away from your family and everyone you loved. I'm sure you were looking around corners the whole time, never being able to rest easy. And to lose the chance to be with your mother in her final days must have been agonizing."

She may not have known the origins of his story, but Violet understood what he'd been through. She felt his pain. It spoke to her compassion and grace, two of the reasons he'd loved her so deeply.

"Living in that state isn't normal. To feel afraid all of the time comes at a high cost," Deacon said. "I never want to go back to that place of fear and panic."

"I know you said that you witnessed two murders that led you into witness protection. I would like to know what exactly happened if it isn't overstepping."

"Of course it's not. I came back here to tell you my truths. Even if Chase has become my main focus."

"I understand," she said, making a tutting sound. "I've had nine years to get used to being his mother. You've only had a few short weeks."

A parent. Suddenly he had a purpose. For so long, he had struggled for a reason to get out of bed in the morning and to keep pushing and striving. Coming to Serenity Peak had given him his reason why.

"I've actually thought a lot about how to tell Chase," Deacon told her. "At his age, he's bound to be curious about what kept me from being in his life. The specifics. Why I was on the run. The way this whole mess started."

Violet frowned, causing a furrow between her brows. "I'd like to hear what you plan to tell him. That way I'll be able to decide whether or not it's something a nine-year-old can handle. That could be fear-inducing. We are talking about a major crime family after all."

"That makes sense. The last thing I want to do is give him nightmares." Deacon shuddered. Over the years, he'd had a few of his own that woke him up in the middle of the night. He'd had a recurring dream in which his mother was calling out to him, only to have her pleas go unanswered. Just thinking about it broke his heart.

"Why don't you come for dinner this evening? We're just having leftovers, but it'll give you a chance to see Chase and for us to talk in private," Violet suggested.

"If you're sure I'm not imposing," Deacon said. He never wanted to feel as if he was a freeloader or an object of pity.

"After all you've been doing to help out around here, that's ridiculous. Your expertise and instincts have made all the difference in getting ahead of this infestation," Violet gushed.

"This place still means a lot to me. Abel always treated me like a son, so I would do anything to make sure Sugar Works continues to thrive."

A beat of silence stretched out between

them. He wondered if Violet was thinking about their past like he was. It was difficult not to when they were working side by side for a common goal, which mirrored the way they had fallen in love with one another.

"I want to make up for lost time," he blurted. Violet's eyes went wide. "With Chase," he quickly added. Adrenaline was still flowing through his body, his heart and mind racing. "I'll come tonight for supper, and I'll bring the dessert. There's a recipe I've been meaning to try out," he said, trying to lighten the mood.

All of a sudden, Violet burst into laughter, her face creased with mirth. She had the type of laughter that was infectious, and he couldn't resist chuckling along with her.

"Deacon! If I remember correctly, you're the worst cook in America. You used to burn everything you attempted to make, even toast."

"Whoa. That's a pretty harsh assessment," he said, trying to keep a straight face. Violet was spot on about his inability to cook. He'd been awful at it, despite his mother's valiant attempts to teach him. Just thinking about his sweet mother caused an ache in his soul. Not a day went by when he didn't miss her.

"As they say, the proof is in the pudding." Violet shrugged. "Prove me wrong."

"You're going to eat your words," Deacon said. "Just you wait," he said, wagging a finger at her. Little did she know that while he'd been on the run he had learned to cook as well as bake. He couldn't wait to surprise her.

Deacon's gaze trailed after Violet as she headed off to another section of the property. There seemed to be a definite thawing between them, so much so that he was reminded of the way things used to be between them. The love they'd once shared had been real and genuine, but it had been a casualty of the Witness Protection Program.

He couldn't get caught up in the memories of their romantic past. His main focus was to bond with Chase and to build something substantial with him while he was here in Serenity Peak. There was nothing between him and Violet but the wonderful son they had created. Everything else was dead and buried.

Deacon couldn't allow himself to get distracted by what might have been. All it would do was drag him under to a place of pain and regret. Been there, done that. Never again, he vowed.

Focus! he urged himself. *Put the past where it belongs. In your rearview mirror!*

When work finished up, Deacon made a quick run to the market before heading back to the inn. He immediately scoured the lobby for Sadie. So far, she had been nothing but good to him. He appreciated

God putting people in his life who encouraged and nurtured him. Sadie was just such a person.

"Sadie, I have a favor to ask," Deacon said as soon as he spotted her by the dining room.

"Ask away. You're one of the best customers we have at the inn," Sadie said with a gentle smile. "You're pleasant, tidy and you never ask for extra towels." She let out a little giggle. "Just a little inn humor."

Deacon chuckled. Sadie was such a sweet woman. Gideon was a truly fortunate man to have her as his wife and soulmate.

"Could I use the kitchen to do some baking?" he asked. He felt a bit sheepish since he already had a bag full of ingredients in his arms. Hopefully Sadie wouldn't think he was being presumptuous.

"Of course you can. You're a baker?"

Sadie asked, her surprise registering in her voice.

This wasn't the first time he'd been greeted with this reaction. At his congregation in Maine, everyone had been shocked when he'd made lemon pound cake for the church bake sale. The truth was that he'd leaned into his baking as a comfort during his time in WITSEC. No matter where he was sent in the country, the two things he could always count on were baking and working as an arborist.

"Over the past few years, I learned to bake. That's what happens when you have a lot of time on your hands," he said, shrugging. "It's been a great hobby."

"Feel free to give Gideon lessons," Sadie said as she led him toward the kitchen. "Everything you need is in the cupboards. Holler at me if you can't find something."

"I sure will," Deacon said as he went about the business of making the best coconut cake he had ever made. He turned the oven to 375 and took out a mixing bowl, a measuring cup and a big spoon. He whistled as he blended the ingredients. He enjoyed the craft of baking more than he'd ever imagined he would. Not only was it a creative endeavor, but he was always less stressed afterward. As soon as he popped the cake in the oven and put the timer on, he headed to his room for a quick shower and a change of clothes.

When he was done, Deacon went back to the kitchen with minutes to spare. When the timer went off, he pulled the cake out of the oven, setting it on the rack to cool down before he could ice it and place the coconut flakes on top.

"Someone's in for a nice treat," Sadie said, standing in the doorway. "It smells incredible."

"Next one is all yours," Deacon said with a wink.

By the time the cake had cooled, he had just enough time to ice it and package it up in a cake holder before heading back to the Drummonds' place. He found himself whistling as he navigated the back roads. His current mood was one of exuberance even though he was dreading telling Chase about the things he'd witnessed in Chicago. Maybe it was too much for a child's ears.

After dinner with the Drummonds, everyone dug into his coconut cake. Soon there wasn't a single morsel left on the platter.

"You made this?" Chase asked between mouthfuls.

"I sure did," Deacon said, feeling amused by the fast rate at which he was devouring the cake.

"Slow down, son," Abel cautioned. "It's not going anywhere other than your belly."

"It's so good you could open up your own shop here in Serenity Peak," Chase said, picking at the crumbs on his plate.

"Now that's mighty praise," Deacon said, sitting back in his chair and grinning. Even though his contribution to the meal had been small, it felt good to be able to give something back to the Drummonds. It didn't feel right to always be on the receiving end of their generosity. Now that his life was more stable, he wanted to provide for his son in a meaningful way. In the future, he would like to help pay his college tuition. *Someday*, he mused.

"I'll clean up the dishes," Skye said, giving Violet a pointed look. "Chase, why don't you help me out."

Chase let out a groan. "Do I have to?"

Ryan came behind him and tousled his hair. "Come on, big guy. The three of us can knock it out in no time. Let's go."

Abel stood up from the table. "That means I can read a bedtime story to the sweetest granddaughter in the world." He scooped Lula up from her high chair and placed her on his hip.

Suddenly, it was just him and Violet sitting at the table. He knew that this had been engineered so that the two of them could talk in private without Chase listening in. Deacon sucked in a deep breath. It was never easy for him to talk about the events that had led to the bottom falling out of his world, but he knew Violet had a vested interest in his story.

And his son was already pressing him with additional questions about what he'd witnessed all those years ago.

Now that he was free from WITSEC, he'd decided to live a life surrounded by the truth. He just hoped that telling that truth was a step forward rather than a huge misstep that Violet would hold against him.

"I figured we could talk in here so Chase can't overhear us," Violet said, closing the den door behind her. "He's at that age where he likes to eavesdrop."

"He may have inherited that from me,"

Deacon said. "Growing up, I got scolded time and again for just that reason."

Violet sat down and motioned for Deacon to follow suit. Sitting so close to him on the love seat lent an intimate vibe to their meeting. "You told me that you were a witness to murder, but could you elaborate a bit? I know it can't be easy for you to talk about, but I'd like to know."

"I was working for my family's landscaping business back in Chicago. That's where I learned everything I know as an arborist. I must have been about twenty-two at the time. The Salomon family was a big deal in Chicago. They owned restaurants, grocery stores and social clubs in the area." He sat back in his seat and fiddled with his fingers. "I went to school with the youngest Salomon son, Nick. We were good friends. Then out of the blue, Nick's father, Gus, offered me a high-paying job at their social club. The money he was offering me was incredible, the type of salary it's hard to say no to." Deacon heaved a tremendous sigh. "I'll admit it, I was blinded by greed and seeking to rebel against what was expected of me. My father was beside himself, and he warned me that they were involved in corruption."

Violet was hanging on to every word Deacon said, riveted by the story. "And I take it you didn't listen to him?"

"Much to my everlasting regret, I didn't. I was at a rebellious age, and I didn't appreciate his wisdom," he admitted. "Things were fine at first, exciting even. Then it got a lot murkier." His jaw clenched. "I overheard conversations that I shouldn't have...about drug shipments and payoffs. Shady people started showing up at the club." He made a slashing motion with his hand. "That was it for me. I wanted out. The very night I planned to quit I went to the club's back office to talk to Gus Salomon. I was in the hallway when I saw Gus and his sons arguing with two men. As the voices became angrier and louder,

I hid in the shadows. I watched as the men were fatally shot by the Salomons. It was the most terrifying thing I had ever seen."

Violet shuddered. "That must have been terrifying. And shocking."

"It was. My whole life turned upside down in an instant," he said, sounding agonized. "These were people I had known my entire life, and up until this point, I trusted them. To see them inflict such violence on human beings was shocking."

"W-what did you do?" Violet asked, her stomach in knots. Deacon was painting such a vivid picture, so much so that she felt as if she'd been there.

"I fled that night without anyone knowing I'd witnessed the murders, but not really knowing what to do," he continued. "But as the days went by, I knew that I had to reach out to the authorities." He looked down at his hands. "Honestly, there are times when I've asked myself if it was all worth it, especially now after finding out about Chase. But I knew that they needed to be stopped before they hurt other people. So I reported what I'd seen that night and became the prime witness in the case against one of Chicago's biggest crime families."

She reached out and touched his hand, squeezing it. "Truth is important. But it isn't fair that you sacrificed so much."

"If I had to do it all over again, I would still testify against them because that's what we're supposed to do. If I hadn't, who knows how many others would have been killed? And it's what brought me here to Alaska."

The door suddenly crashed open to reveal Chase standing in the doorway. His eyes were gleaming, and his hands were fisted at his sides. "I knew it. You're a hero." He came flying across the room, catapulting himself against Deacon's chest.

"I knew there was a good reason you stayed away for so long," Chase cried out. Tears streamed down his face and his body was racked with sobs.

"Chase, what have I told you about listening at doors?" Violet reprimanded him. Despite the emotion of the moment, Chase needed to understand that he'd crossed a line.

Her son glared at her. "I only listened at the door because you never tell me anything. My whole life, you never said one word about my dad. These are things I should know."

Deacon looked down at Chase. "I don't consider myself a hero, son. I'm just a man who wanted to do the right thing." He cupped his hand around the back of Chase's head. "The only thing I regret is that my sacrifice took me away from here. Away from you."

Chase held on to Deacon tighter. He seemed as if he might never let go. Violet wasn't sure she had ever seen him so emotional.

"Chase," Deacon said as he gently disengaged from the embrace. "I wanted you to know what led me into the Witness Protection Program so you would understand how serious the situation was, but I don't want you to be frightened or lose sleep over this. Is there anything you want to ask me?"

"I know you said the bad guys were taken care of, but how? Are they behind bars?" he asked, his lips quivering.

Deacon let out a ragged sigh. "My testimony put the Salomon family in jail."

Chase's mouth hung open. "Even your friend?" Chase asked.

"Yes, Chase. They all went to prison, but they made threats to get revenge against me, which is why I still wasn't safe. They even sent people to come find me, which is why I had to move around a lot. Because they had a lot of enemies due to their criminal enterprise, all of them met their end in prison. They can't hurt anyone ever again."

"Which means the danger is over," Violet said. She needed Chase to know for certain that no one was going to come to Serenity Peak looking for Deacon. She knew how little boys thought about things, and even though he would never admit it, she was certain just hearing the story frightened him.

"Is it?" he asked, looking at Deacon. For a moment, she felt wounded. His entire life, her son had looked to her for affirmation, and now, he was solely focused on his father for reassurance.

"Yes, son, it is. Absolutely. One hundred percent," Deacon confirmed. He put his hands on either side of Chase's face. "That's all in the past. What I want to do from this point forward is focus on the future. And you're at the center of mine."

Chase grinned so hard she thought his face might crack wide open. "Do you want to play checkers before my bedtime?"

"Checkers? How did you know that's my favorite game?" Deacon asked.

"I just had a feeling," Chase said, jumping up and grabbing Deacon by the hand. "We're peas in a pod."

As Violet watched them head off to play checkers, she couldn't ignore the painful hitch in her heart. Why was she feeling left out in the cold? She wanted Chase to have his father in his life after nine years of going without one. And Deacon had been through so much pain. He deserved to have moments of joy with Chase.

Then why did she feel as if she was the odd person out? Why did it seem as if she was losing her son? Things were changing so quickly after being steady for so long. She and Chase never fought, and now they were cross with one another. The dynamic now that Deacon was in the mix was complicated.

She simply didn't know how to feel about Deacon's return and what it meant for her own relationship with Chase.

Chapter Nine

Deacon couldn't quite put his finger on it, but Violet's mood had shifted drastically after their discussion about his past. Was she simply overwhelmed by the way that Chase had dealt with the information? His son's mature manner had totally impressed Deacon. His questions had been full of compassion and insight. Rare in a boy of his age, he noted. It served as further proof of the wonderful job Violet had done in raising him.

When he pulled up in front of the Drummond home the next day, Chase was there waiting for him. Violet walked out the door, looking relaxed in a pair of dark-wash jeans and a white Irish wool sweater. She'd swept her hair up in a high ponytail, showcasing her lovely bone structure and youthful appearance. She still made his pulse race every time she was in his vicinity.

"Hey, Deacon. Thanks for taking Chase on an adventure. He's going to love being there." Although she had a slight smile on her face, Deacon sensed a bit of melancholy in her demeanor.

"What do you have planned for today?" he asked, making small talk.

She shrugged. "Nothing much. Just a few errands to keep me busy."

"Let's go. The dogs are waiting for us," Chase pleaded, tugging on his hand.

Deacon turned toward Chase and asked in a low voice, "Would you mind if I asked your mom to join us? I think she might like that."

For a moment, Chase hesitated. "Sure

thing. I don't mind. We have plenty of time to do father-son stuff, right?"

"That's right," Deacon said. He hadn't thought much about how long he would be staying in Serenity Peak, but he planned to be here for as long as possible. Every moment spent with his son would be making a memory, one that Chase could hold on to for a lifetime.

Deacon turned back toward Violet, who was walking back to the house.

"Hey, Violet," he called out, causing her to turn around. "Why don't you join us?"

"What?" she asked, appearing confused by his suggestion. "No, this is your time with Chase," she said, shaking her head.

"Come on, Mom," Chase said, beckoning her with a wave. "You don't want to miss this. It's all I'm going to be talking about for weeks."

"If you're sure, I'd love to come," she said, holding up a hand. "Give me a second to grab my bag and lock up the house." Without saying another word, she jogged toward the house and disappeared.

Chase looked up at him. "Did you see that smile on her face? You made her really happy. Good job." He held up his hand for a high five, and Deacon happily obliged.

When Violet reemerged, she had a fanny pack around her waist and a sturdy pair of boots on her feet. They all fit in the front of the vehicle, with Violet sandwiched in the middle. Chase was on the hunt for a sighting of a horned puffin, birds that were known to nest near the Halcyon Mountains. With a window seat, he could keep watch in the hopes of spotting the rare bird.

With Violet in such close proximity, Deacon had to work extra hard to focus on the road in front of him. A light lemony scent filled his nostrils. Every time he navigated a curve, Violet's body leaned into his side. He cranked up the radio, praying for a distraction. Violet's honeyed tone filled the truck as she sang along to the tunes.

"You still have a beautiful voice," Deacon noted as he tapped his fingers on the steering wheel in time to the beat. "Do you still sing with the women's choir at Serenity Church?"

"Thanks," she murmured. "I haven't for a while, but I'm considering rejoining. I miss that sense of community."

"That's what I've always loved about this town. It's such a close community," Deacon said. Other than Chicago, there had never been a place where he felt so at home. He just wished that he wasn't getting so many funny looks whenever he ventured around town. It was as if the townsfolk didn't quite know what to make of him. A few times, folks had whispered while looking over at him. That hadn't felt good at all.

"Slow down, Dad. If I have a shot at spotting this bird, it'll most likely be in this area," Chase said, rolling down his window so the brisk air swept over them.

Deacon's heart nearly stopped beating. Had he heard him right? This was the very first time he'd ever addressed him with the *D* word.

"Did he just call me Dad?" Deacon asked Violet in a low voice. He darted a quick glance at her. She was grinning and nodding.

"He sure did. I guess it's official," Violet said. Then she instructed, "Take that right turn at the moose crossing sign. Destiny's place is right by the mountains. Probably about a mile down the road."

Chase began to wiggle around in his seat. "We're getting closer." He let out a little squeal. "This is really exciting."

All of a sudden, the Halcyon Mountains rose up in front of them. They were so close Deacon almost felt as if he could reach out and touch their snowcapped peaks. The only word that came to mind was *magnificent*. Maybe he could take

Chase hiking on one of the trails. As Sean had once told him, the mountains were the most peaceful venue in Serenity Peak. He could use all the peace he could find after so many years of turmoil.

"Turn down this road," Chase shouted, pointing to the red and gold sign that read Destiny's K-9 Dog Farm.

Deacon followed instructions and steered the truck past the welcome sign. Within seconds, the property came into view. A medium-size home with a wraparound porch set against a lush backdrop of woods and mountain. A multitude of dogs were running around in a fenced in area about one hundred yards from the house.

A woman with an athletic frame and shoulder-length dark hair stood by the fence waving at them as they pulled up.

"There she is," Violet said as Deacon turned off the ignition and exited the vehicle.

"Destiny! It's great to see you again,"

Violet said as she stepped down from the truck.

"Violet! I wasn't expecting you," Destiny said, a gentle smile on her face.

"This is my son, Chase, and his father, Deacon," Violet said as she leaned in for a hug.

Deacon held out his hand to Destiny. "We spoke on the phone. Thanks for allowing us to come here today. Chase here is a huge dog lover."

"Well, that makes us instant friends," Destiny said, looking at Chase, who grinned. "I've never met a canine I didn't love at first sight." She spread her arms wide. "Which is why I have this place overrun with dogs."

"You sure do have a lot of them," Chase said, his voice filled with wonder as he surveyed all the dogs racing around. "This place is some kind of wonderful."

"Why thank you, Chase. I consider myself blessed. I also get to help folks who need service animals. That's pretty neat."

"It's really admirable," Deacon said. "Doing good unto others is what life's all about. Or at least it should be." Doing so was one of his major goals now that he was out of WITSEC. So many people had given him a helping hand when he was down and out, especially Abel and Violet. If he could pay it forward to others, Deacon knew it would be rewarding.

"Well, let's take a look around," Destiny said. "I can't wait for you to meet my dogs." She opened the gate and ushered them in as they were swarmed by numerous dogs. Destiny gave the dogs commands that they instantly responded to. There were canines of all varieties— Labrador retrievers, Siberian Huskies, malamutes and a few German shepherds. Deacon wondered how she kept them all straight.

Chase began running around with the dogs, who seemed to enjoy playing with him and all of the attention he was dishing out. When Chase threw a ball, all of the dogs competed to retrieve it. By the time Chase was done, all of the dogs were panting and out of breath.

"They tuckered me out," Chase said, fanning himself. "Destiny, they must keep you on your toes."

Destiny let out a chuckle. "That's for sure. Never a dull moment around here. Why don't we go in the barn where I do some of my training," she suggested. "We have a litter of puppies in there that I'm going to be training soon."

Deacon held the barn door open as Destiny, Violet and Chase filed in. Within seconds, the puppies began making a racket in their enclosure. Tails were wagging, and little yelps were emanating from their direction. A few of the pups got up on their back paws and peeked over the fenced-in area at them. All of the puppies were Siberian Huskies.

"Go ahead and pick one up if you like," Destiny said, leading Chase over.

"This little guy is trying to climb over

the fence," Chase said, leaning over and scooping up the dog. The pup, a gray-and-white Siberian husky, was adorable. Chase immediately cuddled him against his chest. He dipped his head down, earning himself a huge kiss from the puppy before dissolving into giggles.

"He likes you," Violet said, reaching down and patting the dog.

"Are they all in the training program?" Deacon asked. There were seven puppies in the enclosure of varying sizes and coat colors. They were all exuberant.

"This pup here isn't a good fit for the program," Destiny told them, looking at the puppy Chase was holding. "He's smart as a whip, but his temperament isn't quite right for a service dog."

"What'll happen to the little guy?" Chase asked. "Are you going to keep him?"

"Well, I'm hoping someone wants to adopt him and give him a proper home.

But if not, I'll keep him myself," Destiny said. "He's a sweet boy."

"I wish he could be mine," Chase said, swinging his gaze toward his parents. "Can we take him home with us? You know how much I've always wanted a dog." He crossed his hands prayerfully in front of him. "Please, please."

Violet should have seen this one coming as soon as Deacon suggested the visit to Destiny's dog farm. Was she being played by Chase and Deacon, or was this really a surprise turn of events? She wondered if this was why she had been invited along at the last minute.

Feeling slightly annoyed, Violet turned toward Deacon and raised an eyebrow. Was this all a setup?

He held up his hands. "Don't blame me. This is all Chase."

Chase moved closer to her. "Mom, look. He's so innocent and cute. I already know what I want to name him."

"What were you thinking, buddy?" Deacon asked.

"Maverick. It's the perfect name for him. I can just tell he's one of a kind." Chase looked over the moon with joy. She felt tears prick her eyes. As of late he'd been through a lot, and he had been handling it pretty well for a nine-year-old. She was ashamed that she had never given him an inkling about Deacon or prepared him in any way for meeting him. So many years had passed by that she'd convinced herself he wouldn't ever turn up. Thinking that way had made it easy for her to close a door on him.

Violet's heart melted as she watched her son snuggle the puppy. That was the effect he'd always had on her. He made her feel like a mushy marshmallow on the inside.

"So what do you say, Mom?" Chase asked, placing his face next to the puppy's and sending her the sweetest look she'd ever seen.

At a loss as to how to respond, Violet looked over at Deacon. He gave her the slightest nod, letting her know he approved of Chase's plan. Knowing she was outnumbered, Violet let out a sigh of defeat. "Okay. Maverick can come home with us," Violet said, wincing as Chase's earsplitting scream of joy rang out in the barn.

"Careful!" Violet cautioned. "You're going to scare Maverick."

Chase came rushing toward Violet and gave her a tight one-armed hug. In the other, he held Maverick, who seemed content to be in Chase's arms. "This might be one of the best days of my life! I promise that you won't regret saying yes."

"I better not," Violet said, wondering if she had given in too easily. Puppies required a lot of time and attention. They hadn't even figured out who would take care of him while Chase was at school and she was working.

Destiny gathered up a bag of supplies and handed them over to Deacon after he'd made payment. Then Chase put Maverick back in the enclosure with his siblings "Don't worry, Maverick. We'll come back to visit your brothers and sisters."

Violet stood off to the side watching the interplay between her son and his puppy. It really had been love at first sight between them. That helped to ease any niggling worries about whether she'd made the right decision.

Destiny walked over to her, a gentle smile on her face. "Are you okay with bringing the puppy home? You seemed unsure at first," she said. Violet didn't know the woman well, but she sensed her kind nature. She had the feeling that Destiny was a compassionate person who deeply cared about others.

"It'll be fine," Violet answered. "Chase has been begging for one for such a long time now. And his birthday is coming up in a few months, so Maverick can be his early present."

"Caring for a puppy and raising it up is a wonderful endeavor for someone his age." She gently smiled at Violet. "With a little help from Mom and Dad."

With her warm brown skin and light brown eyes, Destiny was a striking woman. Violet knew from past encounters that Destiny was on the shy side. She couldn't recall ever seeing her out and about in town, whereas her older brother, Charlie, was very social.

"You have a beautiful family," Destiny said as she glanced over at Deacon and Chase, who were still playing with the puppy.

"Oh, thank you, but Deacon and I aren't together. Just co-parenting," she explained. That might have been the first time she'd used that word out loud. It would take a little getting used to if she was being honest with herself. She was miles away from the life she'd once dreamed of building with Deacon. Home. Hearth. And family.

"But you're still a family," Destiny said. "That's what really matters."

"You're right," she agreed as the wisdom of Destiny's words washed over her. No matter what had happened in the past between her and Deacon, they would always be a family with Chase at the center, in the present and future. That was something Chase could hold on to forever and always.

When Destiny beckoned Chase over to give him an overview of taking care of Maverick, Violet stepped aside so her son could accept the responsibility of dog ownership. Of course, she would be helping out, but Chase would be doing his fair share of the feeding, walking, bathing and house training. A few moments later, Deacon joined her.

"I promise this wasn't planned," he said. "Scout's honor."

"Were you even a Boy Scout?" she

asked. Deacon didn't give off Boy Scout vibes. Not by a long shot.

He sent her an incredulous look. "For eight long years, I'll have you know. I earned a ton of merit badges along the way." Deacon playfully puffed his chest out, causing her to chuckle.

She glanced over at Chase. He was animated and grinning from ear to ear as he talked to Destiny. "I like seeing Chase so happy. And if getting Maverick keeps him smiling, then who am I to interfere?"

"He has your smile, you know," Deacon said, looking at her with intensity radiating from his eyes.

"And everything else is all you," she teased. It felt nice to finally be able to speak freely about the resemblance between Chase and Deacon. All this time, she'd been so busy shielding Chase from any information about his father. In the end, all she'd done was cause confusion.

He brushed a few strands of hair away from her face, his fingers grazing her cheek in the process. She missed his touch. They had always been demonstrative with one another, whether it was holding hands or tender kisses. Her cheeks warmed at the memory of being kissed by Deacon. Her life had been devoid of any romance since he'd left. Some days, she could barely remember what it had felt like to be loved.

"You haven't changed a bit in all these years," Deacon murmured, his fingers lingering on her face.

His comment crashed over her like a tsunami. She bristled in response. Did he really think that she was the same woman as the one who'd once been in love with him? To her, it felt as if she had lived a few lifetimes since then. Didn't he have a single idea of what she'd endured?

"No, Deacon," she responded in a crisp tone. "Actually, I've changed a lot. Giving birth to Chase and raising him on my own rocked my world. Even if I wanted to, I can't go back to the person I was."

Her lip quivered with emotion. "But you wouldn't know that because you weren't here to see it." She could hear the anger vibrating in her voice, but she couldn't hide how she felt. She had gotten swept up by his involvement in WITSEC and the past he hadn't been able to tell her about. Looking back, she realized how naive she'd been to believe that love was enough to weather any storm.

"Violet, I know it's hard to accept, but I didn't have a choice," he said in a low voice.

"Didn't you? I really don't want to dredge this all up, especially now, but we always have choices. You could have come clean to me and asked me to come with you. Or we could have figured out a solution together. Honestly, I think you simply didn't trust me. And because of that…our son lost out on so much." Her throat was as raw as sandpaper.

Deacon reached out to grab her hand, but she backed away from him. She didn't want to be comforted. Today had been such a nice outing, and then out of the blue, these feelings had swept over her, threatening to swallow her up whole.

"I need some fresh air," she said, walking briskly toward the barn door and pushing it open. Her head was spinning. *Who am I kidding?* It hadn't only been about what Chase had lost out on. She also had been a casualty of Deacon's past.

She was still coming to terms with her own losses, mainly in the form of the man she had just walked away from.

Chapter Ten

Deacon tried to ignore the negative vibes bouncing off Violet on the way back to the Drummond home. Chase was over-flowing with excitement as Maverick nestled in his arms. The puppy slept peacefully for the duration of the ride, which Deacon thought might bode well for his temperament. Hopefully, Chase's nonstop chatter wouldn't disturb the Siberian husky.

Although Violet had every right to speak her truths, he wished they had been alone and able to really talk things through. She had bottled up all of her emotions until they'd come out in a torrent of frustration and anger. Not that he blamed her one bit. There was so much more he yearned to say to her. So many things that were burning up inside of him. He wasn't sure Violet would ever understand the situation he'd found himself in, especially since she had suffered because of it.

Lord, I never thought coming back would be easy, but I also never considered it would be so difficult. Give me the strength to keep trying to make inroads with Violet. It feels like she's drawing further away from me each and every day.

When they got back to the property, Abel was outside the red barn working on a rocking chair. A wooden sign reading Abel's Place hung above the barn doors. He was a talented woodworker who created wonderful pieces in his spare time. He waved to them as they pulled up in front of the two story log-style home. Chase couldn't wait to jump out of the truck.

"Gramps," he yelled. "Look who I brought home."

By this time, both Deacon and Violet had exited the vehicle and were standing nearby.

"What have you got there?" Abel asked, a look of curiosity stamped on his face.

"My very own puppy," Chase exclaimed, holding up Maverick. "Can you believe it?"

"Isn't that terrific?" Abel stroked his jaw and looked over at Violet and Deacon. "You sure are full of surprises. I thought getting a dog was on the back burner."

Violet shrugged, looking sheepish.

Chase turned toward his mother. "Can we set up his feeding area in the kitchen?"

"Why don't we head inside and find the perfect spot," Violet suggested, moving toward the house without looking at Deacon. Chase was fast on her heels.

Ouch! He'd hoped the ride back home would cool her down, but clearly he had been mistaken. He'd been a fool to think things were going smoothly.

"Am I missing something?" Abel asked, his gaze following his daughter. "She seems a bit off."

Deacon sighed. "That's my fault. I unknowingly pushed a few buttons."

Abel made a face. "Don't fret about it too much. It was bound to happen sooner or later. Past hurts have a habit of rising to the surface. Best to deal with them head on." Abel shot Deacon a knowing look.

Abel had always been a truth teller, and now was no exception. Deacon valued the older man's wisdom. During the time he'd previously spent in Serenity Peak, Abel had taught him a lot about life, commitment and hard work. Working at Sugar Works was the type of work he truly enjoyed and he continued to feel grateful.

222   His Secret Alaskan Family

"I've been meaning to ask you something," Abel said.

"Shoot," Deacon answered. He hoped Abel didn't have anything too heavy to lay on him. Deacon already felt a little beaten down from his conversation with Violet.

"With you working for Sugar Works now, as well as needing quality time with Chase, I was wondering if you would consider living on the property. There's an empty house over that hill that's too small for Skye and her family, but it might be just right for you."

Deacon was so surprised he thought his mouth might be hanging open. "Live here? On your property?"

"Yes, Deacon. I know your time here in Serenity Peak might be limited, but the house is yours for as long as you need it."

He was so overwhelmed with gratitude it almost rendered him speechless. "Abel, what a thoughtful offer. I'm blown away to be honest." His chest tightened. "Earlier, Violet reminded me that my situation caused her a lot of pain. I'm not sure she would approve of your idea."

Abel frowned. "I've already run it by Violet, and she doesn't have a problem with it. You know she has a big heart, Deacon. It's as wide as Kachemak Bay."

Violet was one of the sweetest women he'd ever known, which made him ache even more for the pain she had endured on his account.

"Honestly, I'm still trying to figure things out. My original plan was to go back home and help my dad out with his landscaping business. But, of course that was before I found out about Chase. I always want to keep Violet in the loop, no matter what I decide."

"The two of you share a child, and Chase is what matters most."

Abel was right. Living on the property would allow him easier access to his son, and his commute to work would be mere minutes. The offer was a godsend, pure and simple.

"How can I say no?" he asked. "This is truly an answer to my prayers."

Abel placed a hand on Deacon's shoulder. "Then say yes. You've been through a lot, and it's okay to count on folks who want to help you."

Deacon looked down at the ground. "I suppose if I'm being honest, I don't feel worthy of it." Even though he knew he'd been a victim of circumstances and the criminal Salomon family, he still felt responsible for the fallout. He hated the fact that he had been responsible for his family's and Violet's pain.

"Deacon, you're absolutely worthy of good things in this world. You've spent so much time in the darkness. Now you should embrace the light."

"'I am the light of the world; he that followeth me shall not walk in darkness,'" Deacon said. The passage from John was never far from his heart and mind. Now, he just needed to remember that he was worthy of grace.

"I'm glad to see you leaning into your faith," Abel said, grinning. "It will serve you well."

"If I hadn't, I'm not sure that I would have made it through the storms of life," Deacon told him. After losing Violet and leaving Serenity Peak, he'd become un-tethered and despondent, with nothing to lean on. Becoming a man of faith had given him a solid foundation.

"Dad! I want you to see Maverick's pal-let and where he's going to sleep," Chase yelled as he ran toward them. He was so excited that he couldn't seem to catch his breath.

"I can't wait to check it out. And I've got some news for you," Deacon said, looking over at Abel for confirmation. The older man grinned at him. "Guess who's going to be living right over that hill?"

A confused look sat on Chase's face until suddenly his eyes widened. "You? Are you going to be living here with us?"

"Not with you, but close enough that I'll be able to help you out with training Maverick." He winked at Chase. "And now I'll never be late for work."

"Did I tell you that this is shaping up to be the best day ever?" Chase asked as he began running around in circles, letting out little screams of excitement.

Abel looked over at him and grinned. "Something tells me he's pretty thrilled by your news."

Deacon couldn't stop smiling as he watched his son express his joy. This moment felt like his reward for years of suffering. God was good!

When he turned his head, Deacon noticed Violet looking out of one of the first floor windows. Her expression was shuttered, causing him to wonder what she was thinking.

He only hoped that Violet was really okay with him living on the property. If not, then he was walking into a tension-filled situation that could explode in his face.

Violet put her parka on and left the house, deciding to take a brisk walk to Sugar's Place. Although the May weather was warming up from winter, today's temperature sat at thirty-five degrees. Her sister was working in the shop today, and Violet needed a sounding board. She had been stewing since yesterday about her tense conversation with Deacon. Had she been wrong to blow up like that? She knew she'd only been getting her pent-up feelings off her chest, and she had chosen the wrong place and time. It was a blessing that Chase hadn't overheard her. She would have felt so ashamed to put a damper on his big day.

Being honest was important to her,

but she felt guilty about unleashing on Deacon. After all, he hadn't asked to be in witness protection or to be separated from all he'd ever known.

When she rounded the bend and spotted her family's general store, her heart immediately felt lighter. Named after her mother, Sugar's Place was near and dear to her family's heart. The store sold the birch syrup created at Sugar Works, along with soaps, blankets and items of clothing.

A green rocking chair sat on the porch along with a colorful sign inviting customers to come inside. A tinkling noise sounded as soon as the door opened, signaling her arrival. As soon as she stepped inside, the scent of lavender rose to her nostrils. Skye made the loveliest sachets that practically flew off the shelves. She was thrilled that her baby sister had settled into such a nice life with Ryan and Lula.

"Violet!" Skye called out as soon as she spotted her. "I'm so glad you popped in."

"I love visiting this place. Are you busy?" Violet asked. She didn't want to disturb Skye's work day with her impromptu visit.

"No, it's actually pretty quiet today. It seems everyone is gearing up for the Midnight Sun spring festival."

"That's all Chase has been talking about, as well as his new puppy."

"Can't say I blame him. Maverick is all kinds of adorable."

"Where's your little sidekick?" Violet asked, looking around the shop. It wasn't uncommon for Skye to bring her daughter to work with her.

"She's hanging out with her dad today," Skye explained. "Now that she's starting to walk, she's quite a handful when she's here."

"I remember those days," Violet murmured, her eyes misting over. "Cherish them. They go by in the blink of an eye."

"Hey, are you all right?" Skye asked, moving toward her at a quick pace. "Let me make us some tea, and we can catch up."

"Sounds good," Violet said, sniffling.

Within a few minutes, Skye was back with teacups and a kettle. She directed Violet to sit down at the small vintage table that provided a lovely view of the mountains. "I'll be right back with sugar and milk," Skye told her.

Violet poured tea into each cup, and moments later, Skye returned and sat down across from her. They both busied themselves with the sugar and milk.

"So how are things?" Skye asked. "With our schedules, I hardly see you at the house."

A sigh slipped past Violet's lips. "It's been pretty smooth other than a recent hiccup with Deacon."

"Uh-oh," Skye said, raising her cup to her lips.

"Without meaning to, Deacon made a

comment that triggered me. He said that I hadn't changed at all, and all of a sudden I lost it." She set her teacup down with a slight clatter. "Of course I'm different now," she said, unable to hide her annoyance. "Being a single mother has forever changed me."

"Of course it has," Skye said, making a face. "Sounds like he unwittingly opened his mouth and inserted his foot."

"He sure did," Violet said, letting out a huff of air. "In a way, I think he was trying to compliment me, but it just hit me hard. All of these feelings just came out of nowhere," Violet explained. "I can't even properly explain why."

"Violet, I'm going to keep it real with you. You have a habit of keeping everything on the inside. I think you began doing it when we lost Mom so suddenly. You held it all in to be strong for Dad and me." She reached out and squeezed her hand. "I think you need to talk to Deacon without raising your voice or reacting to something he's said. It's never wrong to speak from the heart."

She was quiet for a moment as she absorbed her sister's comment. She knew that she tended to keep her emotions to herself. They had lost their mother due to the flu virus. Losing Sugar had been devastating for all of them. Honestly, she wasn't sure they would ever recover from the shock and the grief. Her mother had been the one to conceive the idea of Sugar Works, yet she hadn't been around to see the birch syrup company come to fruition.

"I don't disagree with you, Skye. When Mom died, I felt as if I had to hold the family together, so I stuffed a lot of my feelings down." She shrugged. "Doing so became my coping technique through the years, especially when my fiancé took off and I found out that I was pregnant."

"It's perfectly understandable," Skye said, nibbling on a tea biscuit. "But you do need to clear the air with Deacon, especially since you're co-parenting Chase."

"When did you get so wise, little sister? I remember the days when you asked me for advice."

Skye let out a chuckle. "Well, as you know, motherhood comes with a huge sampling of wisdom." She raised her teacup and held it in the air. Violet clinked it with her own in a little celebratory gesture.

"Now, don't let this upset you, but the town rumor mill is in full swing." She raised an eyebrow.

"About what exactly?" she asked. While pregnant with Chase, Violet had been on the receiving end of cruel whispers. To this day, it still bothered her. The Serenity Peak community was wonderful, but it only took a handful of people to create negativity.

"Deacon's return." Skye shook her head. "Word got out about him being in the Witness Protection Program, and rumors are swirling that the two of you are at each other's throats. That you think he's putting Chase in danger. Folks have long memories. They're bringing up the incident where the trespasser showed up at Sugar Works with a weapon all those years ago."

"What?" Violet exploded. "This is ridiculous. And the gossip about Deacon and I being at odds is false. I was upset when he first showed up, but we've been getting along fine." And the issues causing tension between them revolved around their former relationship, not around co-parenting Chase.

"Of course it is," Skye said. "I know Ryan and Gideon have gone out of their way to correct folks, but it might help calm things down if the two of you act friendly in public. That way the talk will die down."

Violet made a tutting sound. Hadn't Deacon been through enough? Now he had to deal with being the subject of town rumors. And what if Chase caught wind of the talk? He wouldn't react well to his dad being the subject of unfounded gossip.

By the time Violet left Sugar's Place, the sky was beginning to look cloudy, the threat of a rainstorm on the horizon. Just as she turned down the path, she caught a glimpse of Deacon standing at the front door of his new house. He was waving to her, even from a distance, and he began walking toward her. She placed a hand on her midsection, hoping to calm down the butterflies floating in her stomach as she met him halfway. It was a bit unnerving that Deacon still caused her to feel this way. He was the most handsome man she had ever laid eyes on, with natural-born charisma. She imagined that fact would never change.

"I moved in today. In case I didn't say it before, I appreciate you being on board with Abel's idea," Deacon said. "It's incredibly generous."

"You're welcome. Chase is really stoked about you living nearby. He's planning lots of sleepovers." Between adopting Maverick and Deacon moving into the vacant house, Chase had been in a perpetual state of celebration. Violet hadn't been sure about the move when her father had first mentioned it, but there really hadn't been a valid reason to object. She was learning that her reactions to Deacon were rooted in their past. Letting go of old hurts was complicated.

Suddenly, he seemed nervous. "I don't have a single idea of what goes on at sleepovers. You might need to clue me in," Deacon said, scratching his jaw. "My parents never allowed us to go on them."

It was sweet seeing him so nervous about a simple sleepover. Deacon cared so much about not letting Chase down. He didn't realize that his son was already his number one fan and firmly rooted in his cheering section.

"It's just bonding time really. Games. Food. Movies," she explained. As a young girl, sleepovers had defined her growing-up years. "I would suggest pizza and a Marvel movie. Nothing too scary since he gets nightmares on occasion."

He tapped the side of his head. "I'm taking mental notes. By the way, Chase wants us to go to the Midnight Sun spring festival together." He cleared his throat. "As a family."

She wasn't surprised. For nine years, Chase hadn't had a mother-father unit, and clearly he was eager to show them off to his friends and the townsfolk. His feelings were perfectly reasonable for a boy his age.

"I know you might not want to give folks the wrong idea," Deacon continued, "so I told him that you and I needed to discuss it first."

This was co-parenting in a nutshell. Working together for a common good. A part of her still was getting used to the fact that another person had a say in how to raise Chase. It wasn't just on her shoulders now, which was a relief.

"Actually, I think it's a great idea, Deacon. There's been a lot of whispers about your return. This will give us a chance to show the townsfolk that everything is fine between us with no animosity whatsoever."

"Do you mind telling me what they're saying?" he asked, his gaze narrowing as he looked at her. "I'd like to know."

"Just some foolishness about the two of us not getting along and..." Her voice trailed off as she struggled to find the words.

"What is it, Violet? I can handle it," he said in a low voice.

"They're saying that I think you're going to put Chase at risk with your lifestyle. That having you around could be dangerous for both of us."

He let out a shocked sound. "You've got to be kidding me."

"I wish that I was," she answered, feeling ashamed of the hometown she loved so much. "How can good people act so recklessly? It's cruel. My hope is that Chase never hears any of the whispers."

"Violet, I would never put you or Chase in harm's way. When I said the danger was over, I meant it."

Deacon reached out and took her hand, squeezing it gently. She had always loved the feel of her hand in his. That hadn't changed. Not in all this time.

Stop it! she told herself. This wasn't a romantic encounter between them. They were simply trying to work together for the greater good. The only thing they shared was their son. Maybe if she kept telling herself that, it would sink in.

"We're not going to let this bring us down. I like your idea of presenting a united front for the town. Not only will it give Chase what he wants, but it'll give everyone else an eyeful. As they say, let's give 'em something to talk about."

"And shut down these rumors," she said. "Hopefully for good."

Chapter Eleven

It was quite possible, Deacon thought, that every town resident had shown up for the Midnight Sun spring festival. Crowds of people were gathered around, eating, socializing and snapping their fingers to the lively band. Thankfully, he and Violet had made the sound decision to attend the festivities as a family unit. Abel, Skye, Ryan and Lula had joined them, making it feel more like a family outing.

Chase had been asking a lot of questions about how they'd fallen in love and if they still had feelings for one another. Those inquiries had thrown him for a loop. Out of the mouths of babes. On the ride over, Violet had been very clear in telling Chase that even if his parents weren't together as a couple, they were still a family. For the most part, her words seemed to satisfy Chase, but like most kids his age, Deacon knew this might not be the end of it. He'd also made a point to ask him on several occasions if he was going to be living in Serenity Peak permanently, to which he'd responded that he really wasn't sure yet. At this point, he figured honesty was the best policy.

Chase wasn't the only one thinking about Deacon and Violet's love story. Ever since his return to Serenity Peak, he'd been drowning in memories of his own. Living on the Drummonds' property had only heightened his recollections. His first glimpse of Violet as she tapped birch trees. Walking hand in hand with Violet as she showed him the vast property for the first time. Getting down on bended knee in a grove of birch trees and asking Violet to marry him. Sometimes it seemed as if he was caught in some strange limbo between the present and past.

But, he was determined to be in the moment and enjoy the festivities. It was his first time being out in a public setting with Chase. As soon as they'd arrived, Deacon had noticed that his son was puffing out his chest like a peacock. Clearly, he was excited to show off the fact that his father was present in his life. That knowledge swept over him, creating a little bubble of excitement inside of him. He never wanted to disappoint Chase. The expectations of a nine-year-old boy were sky high.

His stomach grumbled at the aromas emanating from the lineup of food trucks. Roasted chicken and salmon. Fried Oreos and doughnuts. King crab legs. Cotton candy and popcorn. Everywhere he looked options jumped out at him.

Deacon could feel the heat of countless

stares. Although most seemed curious, a few were downright hostile. Some folks seriously needed to get over themselves, he realized. They didn't know his story, or else they lacked even an ounce of compassion. Rather than dwell on it, he decided to turn on the charm, waving and smiling in earnest.

"I see what you're doing," Violet said. "I like your style."

"Kill 'em with kindness," Deacon said, grinning. "Works every time."

"From your lips to God's ears," Violet said, looking around nervously. "This year's crowd seems to be bigger than ever. We've got a lot of eyes on us."

"Hey, this isn't going to work unless you relax. Just think of this as a group outing. Guaranteed fun."

"You're right. I just want everything to go perfectly for Chase." She wrinkled her nose. "At the risk of sounding like a bad mom, it's taken me all these years to realize that he was crying out for a family unit. For a father."

Deacon scoffed. "Violet, you're an incredible mom. Patient and nurturing. Playful and forgiving. And you came upon it honestly. After all, Sugar was an amazing mother to you and Skye."

She turned in his direction. "Thanks for the vote of confidence. I need it right about now."

"Parker!" Chase called out as a boy his size came running toward him at full speed. The boys bumped fists and then began chatting animatedly. Deacon had heard a lot from his son about his best friend, Parker Adams. He and Chase were practically joined at the hip.

"Hey, Chase. Is this your dad?" Parker asked, his eyes focused on Deacon like laser beams. Parker had a head of curly blond hair, hazel eyes and an infectious smile.

"Dad, this is Parker," Chase said. "Parker, this is my dad, Deacon Shaw."

"Nice to meet you, Parker," Deacon said with a nod. "I've heard a lot about you."

"Same," Parker said. "From what Chase said, you're practically a superhero."

They all laughed at Parker's comment, with Abel chuckling the loudest.

"Can we go check out the games?" Chase asked. "Our goal is to win some prizes today."

Parker rubbed his hands together. "That's what I'm talking about."

"I can tag along and keep an eye on them," Abel said with a wink. He tapped his jacket pocket. "Plus I have some money burning a hole in my pocket that they can use to play the games." Parker and Chase let out a cry of delight, and each one grabbed a hold of one of his hands and began tugging.

"I guess that settles it," Ryan said with a chuckle. "I hope Abel can keep up with those two."

Skye looped her arm through his. "Let's

be grateful our daughter is just a toddler in a stroller. Can you imagine racing after her at this event?"

Ryan shuddered. "No, I cannot. Let's head over to the livestock exhibit. Lula is determined to see the goats and lambs."

"We can meet up later and grab some lunch. Keep your ringer on," Skye called out as they headed off to the animal display.

"And then there were two," Deacon said as he stood with Violet, watching the others disperse.

If he was being honest with himself, he enjoyed being alone with her. Sooner or later he hoped that he could have a completely honest conversation with her where they were able to show their vulnerabilities without anger or recrimination. He wasn't sure she completely trusted him yet. Perhaps it was a bridge he needed to build with her.

"You won't believe this! Come and see," Violet said, tugging on his arm and leading him toward one of the food trucks. She grinned at him. "Betcha never imagined you'd see one of these in Alaska. Ta-da," she said, holding her arms wide open in front of a brightly colored shaved-ice truck. The sight of it caused Deacon to laugh out loud.

"Shaved iced? Hilarious," he said, slapping his leg with his hand. "This means we absolutely have to get some. My treat."

"I'll never turn down sweet treats," Violet said, studying the flavors. They stood in line, and when it was their turn, Violet ordered the bubblegum flavor while Deacon picked blue coconut.

He shivered as the cold treat practically made his forehead tingle. "Brain freeze." He choked out the words, causing Violet to giggle.

"Come on," she said, still laughing. "It's not that bad."

"Speak for yourself," he said. "You Alaskans are used to arctic temperatures."

"Well, I'll never forget our first date. You wanted to take me out for ice cream after dinner." Her eyes twinkled as she spoke.

"Yes, or at least I tried. Who knew it would be so hard to find an ice cream parlor here?" Deacon asked. In the end, they had headed over to Northern Lights for some amazing pie Sean's sister had made. It was so good Deacon could almost taste the berry flavor on his tongue.

"We had some fun times, didn't we?" she asked. Her expression was thoughtful, almost as if she too had taken a walk down memory lane.

"The best times of my life," he said. And that was the truth. Although he loved his family back in Chicago, nothing compared to the months he'd spent with Violet. Falling in love with her had changed his life. After the ordeal with the trial and being hunted by the Salomon family, she had given him hope and a sense of purpose. A future to look forward to.

Violet looked up at him, surprise registering in her eyes. Did she truly not know how deeply he treasured their time together? Although she wasn't saying so, every instinct told him she felt the same way. The past still stood between them, a huge chasm. He felt it in every single one of their interactions. What would it take, he wondered, for her to peel back her layers?

"Are you aware that Chase plans to stay until midnight?" Deacon asked, changing the subject. The Midnight Sun spring festival was an all-day affair, continuing until midnight.

"That's a good one. Absolutely not," she said with a firm shake of her head. "I think he's trying to pull one over on you. He's trying to test your parenting rules."

"Hmm. I thought midnight was kind of pushing it," Deacon said. "I'm learning day by day that kids are way craftier than I realized."

Just then they reached the Northern Lights table, manned by Sean and his younger sister, Cecily. The awning advertised Pies by Cecily. Deacon had only a vague recollection of Sean's youngest sister, but he was intrigued by her pies. There were a variety of flavors on display—berry, apple, peach and rhubarb. The way people were lining up to buy them was a great indicator of their popularity.

Violet gave him a nudge. "Cici's pies are terrific," she told him. "They always sell out at Northern Lights."

"Thanks for the praise, Violet," Cici said. "I like waitressing at Northern Lights, but baking pies is my passion. I learned pie making from my mom." She leaned in and whispered, "Don't tell my big bro, but I'm thinking of setting up my own shop." Cici looked a lot like

Autumn, but she was more petite with a mane of curly hair.

"Hey," Sean said, "you're my secret weapon at the restaurant. You can't leave me high and dry."

Cecily rolled her eyes at her brother.

"By the way, we've never officially met, but your name has been on the tongues of a lot of my customers," Cecily said with a knowing look.

Since Cecily was so jovial, Deacon didn't get his back up about her comment. He liked when people didn't skirt the truth.

"Between you and me," he whispered back, "I had that feeling ever since I arrived in town." He let out a low chuckle. She laughed along with him.

Sometimes a person just needed to let things go and not dwell on them. Focusing on negativity would only bring him down, and he couldn't allow that to happen.

This too shall pass, he told himself. No

small-town gossip could get him to leave his son after being separated for such a long time.

When they met up with Chase and the rest of Violet's family, he and Deacon went off together to check out a demonstration by Ace Reynolds, a former Iditarod racer. Ace was married and had settled in Owl Creek, working alongside his veterinarian wife, Maya, with rescue dogs. Now that Chase had his own dog, he was deeply interested in Ace's mission. It was safe to say that Chase was in his dog era.

After spending some time learning about rescue dogs and meeting the famous musher and his wife, he and Chase rejoined their group at the stage.

"That was really cool, Dad," Chase said, grabbing hold of his hand. "This is the best festival ever so far. Do you want to know why?"

Deacon nodded. "Of course." He felt a lump forming in his throat.

"Because I'm with you," Chase said, confirming what Deacon had thought he was going to say.

Words couldn't describe this feeling. Without a doubt, this was love unlike anything he'd ever known. It hummed and pulsed inside his chest every time his son was nearby. He hadn't been prepared for this tidal wave of emotions.

"I know, buddy. I feel the same way," Deacon said, somehow managing to get the words out. He squeezed his son's hand as they headed back to the stage where the band was playing a lively set.

He was busy blinking back tears, ones that were a result of joy and not sadness.

Violet clapped her hands to the beat of the live band as she stood with her father, Skye, Ryan and Lula. The band was terrific, playing upbeat rhythms that made her want to cut a rug. She couldn't remember the last time she'd actually been on a dance floor. And it was such a shame since she loved to dance.

Although she had devoted her life to raising her son and being second-in-command at Sugar Works, moments like this reminded her of all the things that were missing.

She looked around, wondering why Chase and Deacon were taking so long. Normally Chase was glued to her side at this festival, but these days his focus was on his friends and Deacon. She didn't want to begrudge Deacon spending quality time with Chase, but as of late, she felt as if everything in her life was spinning out of control.

All of a sudden, Deacon and Chase appeared with smiles on their faces and huge turkey legs in their hands.

"There you are," Violet said, greeting Chase with a kiss on his forehead. "I was wondering where you were."

"I met Ace Reynolds, and he's really

cool," Chase said. "Want some?" he asked, holding out his turkey leg.

Abel took it out of his hands and said, "Don't mind if I do. Walking around works up an appetite."

"Let's dance," Ryan said. Holding Lula against his hip with one arm, he grabbed Skye's hand and pulled her to the dance floor. "This music is too good to waste."

Ryan is right, Violet thought. A passage from Ecclesiastes came to mind. *A time to weep and a time to laugh; a time to mourn and a time to dance.*

"How about it?" Deacon asked, holding out his hand to Violet. "Care to take a spin?"

Just watching everyone else on the makeshift dance floor inspired her to say yes. *What would be the harm?* she asked herself. Deacon was waiting for an answer while Chase was watching with big eyes.

"Go on, Violet," her father urged, gently nudging her with his elbow.

Violet reached out and slid her hand into Deacon's, her skin tingling at the contact. Before she knew it, Deacon had swept her onto the dance floor and into his arms. As the music slowed down, Deacon pulled her against his chest. A woodsy scent rose to her nostrils. Despite the fact that it had been a decade since they'd danced, Violet felt as if she was floating. As she laid her head on his shoulder, it struck her that this all felt so effortless.

Being held in Deacon's arms shouldn't feel so natural after all this time, yet somehow it did. His strong arms around her waist provided a sense of warmth and security. At the same time, it scared her. Feeling so in tune with him was surreal. She didn't want to dwell too long on what it could possibly mean. So far she had avoided examining her feelings for Deacon too closely. But with each day that passed, it was getting harder and harder.

When the band stopped playing to take a break, Deacon led her back to where they'd left the others, only to find that they were no longer there. Violet figured that Chase had taken his grandfather to another vendor's stall or to see an exhibit. As they all knew, Chase had Abel wrapped around his little finger. The crowd around the stage was beginning to thin out, so they had a clear view of the area.

Deacon looked around. "Left to our own devices it seems."

"Maybe Chase cringed at the sight of his parents dancing," Violet teased. She was hoping to tone down the intimate vibe that had been brewing between them on the dance floor. She wondered if Deacon had experienced feelings similar to her own. Violet had no idea what he had been up to over the last decade, and she hadn't wanted to ask. Had he been in love with anyone else? Did he have someone special in his life?

She drummed up her courage and asked, "So Deacon, is there someone waiting for you back in Seattle? Or Chicago?"

"No, I'm single. I'm not very good at making those connections," he told her. "Chase made a point of telling me that you were too, so I assume that's true." Their gazes met and Violet nodded.

"It is," she said. "I never managed to juggle motherhood and romance. Sure, I've been on a few dates, but those relationships never went very far." That was an understatement!

"It's a little strange for both of us since we intended to settle down with one another," Deacon said. "It's hard for me to imagine you walking through life alone."

"Oh, I haven't been alone for a single moment. With Chase, my family and close friends, I've had a full life." Her tone may have sounded a bit brusque, but she didn't want Deacon to pity her for a life she loved. It was one she'd built after disappointment and challenges, but it was hers. Perfectly imperfect. And wonderful.

He clenched his jaw. "I've struggled with surrounding myself with a support system," he admitted. "It's difficult for me to open myself up to people. I think it was hard for me to get past what we shared. Violet, I sincerely wanted to spend the rest of my life with you." A vein pulsed by his eye. "I knew proposing to you might not be fair considering the secrets I needed to keep, but I had to follow my heart."

"You don't owe me an explanation," Violet said. "The situation you found yourself in was extraordinary."

"I'm simply speaking my truths," he said, looking at her with an intense expression.

"I respect that," Violet said. And she did. She simply wasn't sure she could withstand talking about their romantic past. It had all crashed and burned when he'd left town. After all these years, Violet wasn't over the dissolution of the dreams that had been tied up in Deacon. Their life together could have been so beautiful if circumstances hadn't kept them apart.

"Maybe Chase would benefit from knowing more about our past. Regardless of how things ended, it was a love story," Deacon said.

"I don't know, Deacon. Maybe it's best not to fill his head with all of that. It was a lifetime ago. Some things are better left unsaid." She folded her arms across her chest. Deacon was getting too close now to the wounded part of her soul that she kept locked away from prying eyes. It would be too painful to dredge it all up.

Talking with their son about the past she and Deacon shared would be like inviting all the sweet memories to envelop her. And that would be too dangerous. She couldn't allow herself to get swept away by a host of memories.

As it was, Violet was already on shaky ground. She was jittery. And she couldn't help but feel that she might just fall on her face.

Chapter Twelve

Why did I agree to dance with Deacon? It had been a step too far. Too close. Too intimate. As a result, she was now a bundle of nervous energy. Being physically close to him always did a number on her. She should have known better than to put her fingers too close to the fire.

"Deacon, please," she said. "Things are just going too fast at the moment. I need everything to slow down a bit." She turned her head away from him, afraid to look in his eyes. She was incredibly vulnerable to him and everything he represented. Romance. Love. Happily-ever-after. Bringing up their romantic past was sending her into a tailspin.

Deacon gently pulled her to a quiet area behind the stage, away from prying eyes. With emotions running high, she was thankful for the privacy. This was the last thing she wanted the townsfolk to gossip about.

"Talk to me, Violet, the way you used to. Open up. I want to know about your life since I've been gone. I knew you inside and out when we were engaged, but who are you now?"

The tone of his voice was tender, and for a moment she almost forgot that there was nothing between them anymore except their son. Everything they'd established had been erased over time, swept away by outside forces that had been out of their control. Whenever she thought about all they had lost, it made her ache inside. Because he was right. They had shared a love story for the ages.

"That was a long time ago," she said,

steeling herself against the onslaught of memories. More and more she was softening toward him, leaning into the man she had once loved. She'd tried to keep a wall up between them in order to protect herself, but it was beginning to crumble.

"But it still was love," Deacon said. "We can't erase what we meant to each other."

"What do you want me to say?" she exploded. "That I cried so hard when you left that I broke blood vessels in my eyes? That I looked for you every single day for months, hoping you would return? That I bugged Gideon for weeks thinking something had happened to you?

"And when I found out I was pregnant with our child, all I felt was sheer panic. I've never experienced such loneliness in my life or a feeling of such despair." She let out a sob, and tears streamed down her face. She didn't even bother wiping them away. If Deacon wanted to see her vulnerabilities, then here they were, all laid out for him. She wasn't a pretty crier, so she knew he was getting an eyeful.

He took a step toward her, easily closing the distance between them.

"Violet, if I'd known, I would have come back in a heartbeat. I would have risked it all just to be at your side. It would have been the honor of my life to raise Chase with you." He reached out with his thumb and wiped away some of her tears. "I never want to see you cry. It rips me up inside."

Her body was trembling uncontrollably. At this point, she just needed to let everything pour out of her. She had been holding it in for far too long. "I'm strong in public and in front of Chase, but in private I've shed a lot of tears. My whole life changed on a dime when you left town. I went from planning our wedding to having to mourn the loss of you. Except you were alive as far as I knew."

All of her tortured emotions from that time came rushing back to her, threatening to swallow her up whole. At the time, she had only confided in Autumn and Skye, but Violet hadn't wanted to lay it all on their shoulders. Her small world had felt like such a lonely place.

"You know how much I love this town, but I was the subject of cruel whispers and gossip. I'm a strong woman, but a person can only withstand so much before crumbling. But I'm proud to say that I got back up, wiped my tears away and got about the business of living and raising our son. Because no matter how badly I was hurting, Chase needed me to show up each and every day. In my heart, that's who I am. A mother."

He caressed her cheek with his palm, the movement soothing and grounding. His touch was like a healing balm.

His deep hazel eyes radiated compassion. "This is about you right now, but please don't think my heart wasn't broken too. You have no idea how many times I wanted to turn around and run right back to you."

"Why didn't you?" she asked him, the words flying out of her mouth. Things might have turned out so differently if he'd done so. Chase would've had a father. And she would've had the love of her life.

"I didn't come back for the same reason that I left. The threat of danger hadn't gone away. The Salomons were monitoring my parents' calls. After I reached out to my mother, they sent someone to find me. That trespasser at Sugar Works came for me. And I couldn't risk putting you in the crosshairs. That's how much I loved you."

Violet's heart thumped noisily in her chest. Suddenly she felt weightless. Deacon's love had always lifted her up to the stratosphere. She couldn't pretend there hadn't been a huge void in her life with his absence. Nothing and no one could have filled it up other than Deacon himself.

"No matter what, I'm happy that you and Chase were safe." He swept his thumb across her cheek. "That helps me sleep at night."

"Oh, Deacon," she said, looking up at him through a veil of tears.

"Violet," he murmured, dipping his head down and placing his lips solidly over hers in a kiss that made her go weak in the knees.

Kiss her. The words bounced off his brain like a rubber ball, urging him to act. This wasn't the first time he had been tempted to kiss Violet, but so far he'd managed to stuff those feelings down. Until now. One look in her eyes and he'd fallen headfirst into this incredible moment. And he didn't regret it for a single instant.

Violet tasted like cotton candy as he moved his lips over hers. Pure sweetness! As she returned the kiss with equal measure, Deacon felt something humming in the air around them. He placed his hands at the back of her neck, anchoring her in the kiss. Her hands tightly gripped his arms. A sweet vanilla scent assailed his senses, and her long hair swept across his cheek. He could hear the thrumming of his own heart pulsing in his ears.

How many times had he dreamed of this moment over the years? A thousand times or more perhaps. It was way sweeter than he'd ever envisioned. Deacon wanted to shelter Violet from all the pain and heartache of the past. He yearned to provide a soft place to fall so that she would never feel alone again.

As the kiss ended and they broke apart, Deacon continued to rain little kisses on Violet's lips. He really didn't want this moment to end. It was like seeing the northern lights shimmering in an Alaskan night sky. Powerful and mesmerizing.

This kiss left him breathless.

Violet ran her fingers through his hair,

her movements gentle and tender. Their gazes locked and held. What he saw radiating from her eyes wasn't reassuring. She looked bewildered, as if she wasn't quite sure how they'd gotten to this place.

"We should rejoin the others," she murmured, a slight frown marring her face. "If Chase had come looking for us, he might have gotten an eyeful."

"I don't like this little frown here," he said, touching the space between her brows. "Are you all right?"

"Oh, Deacon," she said, running a finger across her lips. "I'm just not sure we should have shared that kiss. Things are complicated enough as it is."

Ouch. The little bubble of joy that had been floating inside of him abruptly burst. After all this time, he'd felt as though the door was opening between him and Violet, only to have it slammed closed in his face. Violet's expression spoke volumes. She regretted their kiss, and he didn't quite know what to do now. His ego felt slightly bruised.

Shake it off, he urged himself. She might be right, despite how good it had felt to kiss her. Their focus was Chase. He'd hurt Violet enough for three lifetimes. Why would she ever want to revisit that chapter of her life? Even though she was allowing him to build a relationship with their son, it didn't mean she was welcoming him into her life.

Clearly, that ship had sailed. And he shouldn't even have taken a risk, knowing that it could complicate an already fragile situation.

"I understand," he told her. "Going down that road is complicated given our past relationship."

"It is," Violet said. "And I know your focus is centered on Chase, which is where it should be. You've lost so many years together."

They were both silent for a moment, as if each of them was thinking about where to go from here. A slight tension hung in the air, no doubt fueled by the misguided kiss.

"Speaking of which, we should go round him up," Violet said, fidgeting with her necklace. "He needs to go check on Maverick and feed him."

So far, Chase had been doing a bang-up job of caring for his new puppy. Although he hadn't had him for very long, his dedication to the pup was commendable.

"Let's go," he said, knowing that they were both walking away from this tender moment and drawing a line in the sand. Once again, he was experiencing another loss.

When they rounded the corner, Deacon easily spotted Chase. "There he is," he said, leading Violet in their son's direction. As they drew closer, Deacon saw Chase engaged in a loud argument with a boy his age. Abel was holding Chase back as he flailed his arms and attempted to break free from his grandfather's grasp.

"Chase!" Violet called out as they both raced to his side.

"Take it back," Chase yelled, his face mottled with anger.

"What's going on here?" Deacon asked, standing between the boys. A group of kids had gathered around to watch the spectacle.

"Chase didn't start it," Parker spoke up. "Ethan did." He pointed to the other boy.

Abel shook his head. "Everything was fine, until they started shouting and shoving each other. I can't figure out what's going on."

Deacon crouched down and looked into his son's face. "Calm down and talk to me. What's this all about?"

Abel let go of Chase and began to disperse the crowd of boys.

Chase's lip trembled uncontrollably. He was breathing choppily through his nose. "H-he was talking smack about you." He was looking directly at Deacon, leaving no doubt as to who he was talking about.

"Take it easy. You know better than to listen to nonsense or act out like this," Violet chided. She sounded incredibly disappointed.

"He said that my dad was a criminal," Chase said, his voice breaking. "And that the reason he was gone all my life was because he was in jail."

Deacon's heart skittered. Seeing his son so upset because of him was heartbreaking. He reached out and grasped Chase by his arm in an effort to console him. Chase turned to Violet and buried himself against her chest, heaving huge sobs. The rejection hurt more than he even wanted to admit to himself. He wasn't the parent that Chase turned to for comfort. It was a painful realization. Had he lost too many years with his son that he couldn't ever make up for?

As they made their way to Abel's van after deciding to call it a night, Deacon tried to come up with something to say to make Chase feel better. The sticks-and-stones speech wouldn't work in this situation. He hated that his son was hurting because of him. He didn't think he'd ever felt so useless in his life.

Violet sat in the back seat with Chase, her arms around him, comforting him while Deacon helplessly looked on. Chase wasn't even making eye contact with him. His presence in town was making Chase's idyllic life way more complicated. The question relentlessly nagged at him. His original plan had been to return to his family in Chicago. Finding out about Chase had complicated things. At this point, he found himself at a crossroads. Should he stay in Serenity Peak or head home to Chicago?

Chapter Thirteen

Violet closed Chase's bedroom door behind her and let out a ragged sigh. For a moment, she leaned against the wall and listened for any signs of distress. Hopefully her son would fall fast asleep rather than tossing and turning in his bed.

Lord, please watch over Chase. Hold him in the palm of Your hand and see him through this moment. This too shall pass.

Their fun outing had ended on a sour note, which was a shame for everyone, especially Deacon and Chase. She knew from the troubled expression on Deacon's face that he was gutted by the turn of events. Coming back to Alaska had been an emotional ride for Deacon, and her heart went out to him. Being a parent was tough in normal circumstances, but to suddenly find out one was a father was head spinning.

When she made her way back downstairs, Deacon was pacing across the hardwood floors in the foyer. He glanced in her direction at the sound of her footsteps on the stairs.

"How's he doing?" he asked. "He seemed pretty upset."

"He'll be fine. I'm sure it'll all blow over." She blew out a huff of air. "It's just ridiculous that adults spread ridiculous gossip that kids overhear and repeat. Shame on them for even going down that road!" Elders had a responsibility to set an example for the children in the community. She couldn't help but feel that many were failing to do what was right. It was incredibly disappointing to see this happening in such a wonderful place as Serenity Peak.

"I can't help but feel that this falls on my shoulders," Deacon said. At that moment, Skye walked in the room bearing steaming mugs for both of them.

"I thought you could use some chamomile tea," Skye said, placing the cups down in front of them on the coffee table. "Try not to worry too much about Chase. He's strong, like his parents."

"Thanks, Skye," Deacon said. "This is perfect."

"I appreciate the support," Violet said, raising her mug to her lips.

As soon as Skye left the room, Violet tried her best to turn Deacon's mindset around. "With regard to what you were saying before Skye came in the room, I thoroughly disagree with you. None of this is your fault." She was regretting all of her reservations about Deacon bonding too fast with Chase. So far, she had seen nothing but positivity flowing from his direction. He didn't deserve this!

"It feels like I'm the source of his pain and embarrassment. He wouldn't even look at me," Deacon grumbled. His jaw was clenched tightly while harsh lines creased his forehead. He was definitely taking this to heart.

"Being a parent is a marathon, not a sprint. There are going to be pitfalls along the way, but you need to keep the faith and stay committed to your role as his father." She stirred her tea and added some sugar. "I have your back, Deacon."

"I just wish there was something that I could do to calm down the gossip. What if it continues to swirl around at school?" he asked, sounding agonized. "When I first returned, you wanted to shield Chase from my presence. Maybe your first instinct was correct."

"That was before I knew about all the reasons why you stayed away. Plus, I was frightened."

His eyes widened. "Of me?"

"No, of what your return could mean. Not just for Chase, but for me as well. It would mean I had to step up and tell our son about you. I should have told him about you a long time ago, and I didn't." She met his curious gaze. "It was wrong of me, regardless of how you left. Every child has a right to know where he came from."

"I agree," he said, nodding. "But… I don't know. It just feels like something was broken tonight. Before Chase was looking at me through rose-colored glasses. Tonight it seems as if someone smashed those glasses, and he's now seeing me differently."

"He's nine years old. Of course he views you as a superhero. You're all fresh and new and exciting. That was bound to wear off a little," she explained. "But Chase adores you. He's not going to let some idiotic rumor change the way he feels about you. Was it an uncomfortable moment? Yes. Was it enough to derail your relationship? Of course not."

"You really think so?" he asked, sounding uncertain.

"I know so. My advice for you is to just keep building those bridges with Chase. He's really excited about helping you decorate your new digs, so that would be a great way to keep things in a positive zone."

"That's a great idea," Deacon said. "I have some pictures to hang up and a little painting to do, so he could be my sidekick."

"Exactly," Violet concurred. "It will make him feel grown up."

"I better head out," Deacon said, standing up. "I've got to get up at the crack of dawn tomorrow to help tap the syrup."

"Me too," Violet said. It was nice that she and Deacon were both working at Sugar Works. She stood up and followed him down the hall to the front door.

Just as Deacon touched the doorknob,

he turned toward her and said, "Thanks for all the support. I'm not sure I would have made any inroads at all with Chase if it hadn't been for you."

"Are you kidding me? You had him at hello. I've never seen someone fall for someone so fast," she teased.

Deacon grinned down at her, causing a little hitch in her heart. "Night, Violet."

"Night," she said as he opened the door. All of a sudden, he let out a gasp as the sky lit up in a brilliant display of vibrant colors—greens, blues and purples.

"I don't believe this," he said as he stepped outside. "The aurora borealis. At last."

She grabbed her jacket and followed behind Deacon, not wanting to miss this epic moment. Catching a glimpse of the northern lights was serendipity.

"Wow. This isn't something one can predict," she said, looking up at the undulating lights in the night sky. "You have to catch them just at the perfect moment."

"I've never seen them before," he said, sounding awestruck. "Not during the time I lived in Alaska or anywhere else. This is definitely a bucket list moment. I can't believe I get to witness this breath-taking sight after all these years."

Violet understood his emotion. She had seen this glorious sight dozens of times in her life, but it never got old. This was Deacon's first sighting, which made the moment even more precious. Violet looked over at him, enjoying the way his gaze was single-mindedly focused on the northern lights. He was such a man of strength, she realized. It never ceased to amaze her how he remained so hopeful after life had handed him so many lem-ons.

"It's like the lights are dancing for us," she said. "I wish that you could experi-ence this with Chase."

He looked over at her, his hazel eyes skimming over her face. "There'll be plenty of time for that in the future, but

I happen to think this moment is unfolding just the way it should."

They were standing so close Violet could see the tiny freckles on the bridge of his nose and the little scar by his eye. Every time they were together like this, it seemed as if nothing had changed, yet in reality, she knew better. They had spent a decade apart. It wasn't possible to simply pick up where they'd left off.

But they still had an undeniable connection. There was that push and pull between them. She sensed he felt it as well. She felt closer to him than she had ever imagined possible.

Once again, Deacon was part of her world, and she really couldn't imagine her life without him in it. The realization was stunning. And even though she had expressed regret over their earlier kiss, Violet yearned to kiss Deacon again. There was no way on earth she could stop her heart from opening itself up to him.

Despite her best intentions, she was falling for Deacon all over again.

Working at Sugar Works occupied most of Deacon's time over the course of the next few weeks. It was birch tapping season which meant all hands on deck for harvesting the trees for product. Now that the company was fully staffed again and the birch borer crisis was over, he'd thought that things would slow down a bit. He'd been wrong. Operations were going at full speed, which kept him incredibly busy. Sugar Works had grown over the last decade, with more workers, increased production and larger distribution.

Ever since the night that he and Violet had caught a glimpse of the northern lights, she had been missing in action. While Abel had told him she'd gone to Kodiak on business, he couldn't help but wonder if she was avoiding him. She had made her feelings clear about regretting their kiss, which had been tantamount to holding up a stop sign. He wasn't the type of man who would ever push for something more than Violet wanted to give. Accepting that their love was in the past was a bitter pill to swallow. Perhaps all this time he'd been harboring the notion of a romantic reunion between them.

The truth was, he didn't deserve a woman like Violet. He'd never been worthy of her goodness. He didn't know why he had even proposed to her back in the day.

Because you loved her, a little voice in his head reminded him. Truly. Deeply.

His emotions were hard to stuff down. Kissing her hadn't just been an impulsive gesture for him. Doing so had shown him that his heart was still wrapped up in Violet Drummond. Sweet, caring Violet. Had he truly ever gotten her out of his heart and mind? The answer was clear to him. She had imprinted herself on him like a tattoo. For life. He couldn't imagine not feeling this way about her, which would make being in her presence all the more painful. Not only was he working at her family's company, but he was living on Drummond property. Perhaps he had made a mistake on both fronts.

Today, Chase was coming over to his place to help him set up and make the house more comfortable and eye-catching. He wanted to decorate the guest room with Chase's favorite things, which at the moment seemed to be dogs and a popular cartoon character. When Chase showed up around ten that morning, he was full of excitement.

"This is going to be an awesome man cave!" Chase said, looking around the living room and den area with awe.

Deacon chuckled. "Back up, son. That's not what we're calling it. And please don't pass that on to your mother." He was still earning his dad stripes, and he didn't want Violet questioning anything about his parental role.

Chase looked disappointed. "Okay, but can I call my bedroom that?"

A smile twitched at his lips. "Go for it."

Chase was a hard worker, and he set about the business of helping Deacon paint his room a vivid blue. Peacock blue as Chase described it. Once they were done, they cracked open a window for ventilation and closed the door behind them.

"How long until I can sleep in there?" Chase asked. He was practically bouncing off the walls with excitement.

"A week to be on the safe side." He tousled his son's head of curly dark hair. "We don't want those fumes to scramble your brain."

Chase made a goofy face and let out a boisterous laugh. He rubbed his hands together. "What's next? The living room?"

"Sure thing. I bought a rug and a coffee table that we can set up in front of the television. And I picked up some throws for the couch."

"Let's get cracking then," Chase said, leading the way to the storage area. By the time they were done, the area looked not only habitable, but fashionable as well. He had also hung up a few pictures of Chicago and one of Kachemak Bay.

"Are you going to take me to Chicago so I can meet my other grandpa?" Chase asked.

"I'd love to take you to my hometown if that's something you're interested in." Just the thought of showing Chase around Chicago was thrilling. He would love for his son to see him through the lens of the town he'd grown up in.

"Of course I am. I've heard that deep dish pizza is the best." He rubbed his hand over his tummy.

"You don't know the half of it," Deacon said, putting his hand to his lips in a chef's kiss gesture. "I'm going to take you to the place my pops always took us when we were your age. Giordano's. We'd go to Wrigley Field for a baseball game, then dinner at Giordano's." He didn't want to bust up the mood by telling his son that he might just be living permanently in Chicago.

Chase let out a little squeal. "When can we go? I'm ready now."

"I need to talk it over with your mom first," Deacon told him. "To be honest, I'm not sure how she'll feel about that."

His son frowned. "Why? She's all about family ties, and I want to meet your side of the family."

"Well, a lot of bad stuff happened to me in Chicago, and as a mom, that weighs heavily on her mind." He placed his hand on Chase's shoulder. "I know for a fact the danger is over, but the idea of taking you there might not be that appealing to her. It might scare her."

A thoughtful expression came over Chase's face. "I get it. So I'm going to make a huge list of all the reasons I need to go to Chicago and give it to her. That'll win her over."

"I like the way you think, hotshot. How about some pizza for dinner? We can ride into town to pick it up."

"Say less," Chase said, running toward the coat rack and grabbing his coat.

Deacon called in their order so it would be ready by the time they arrived. When they came back to the house with the pizza, Violet was standing at his doorstep.

"Sorry if I'm early. I may have gotten the time wrong," she said, sounding apologetic.

Deacon looked at his watch. "Sorry. It's my fault. I lost track of time with all the painting and decorating we did."

"We worked up an appetite," Chase said, holding up one of the pizza boxes.

"I'll come back in an hour or so," Violet said, turning away from the house.

"Stay and eat with us," Deacon said impulsively. They hadn't shared a meal together, just the three of them. He was constantly being reminded that they were a family, despite the fact that he and Violet were no longer together. Chase needed to know that his parents got along and weren't at each other's throats.

"A-are you sure? I know this is your time with Chase," she said. "I don't want to intrude."

"Mom, we can't eat two pies between us," Chase said, motioning to the door with his chin. "Come on in." Deacon loved how his son was acting as if it was his home as well.

"I'd love to," Violet said, a smile lighting up her face. She opened the door and held it so that Deacon and Chase could enter with the pizza boxes in hand. Chase led the way toward the kitchen and placed his box on the butcher-block table.

"Good thing I just picked up some chairs," Deacon said with a chuckle. "Sadie, bless her heart, was kind enough to give me some from the inn that she wasn't using."

Violet looked around. "Everything

looks great. All you need are some curtains and a splash of color to make it
more homey."

"You're welcome to come help decorate," Deacon teased. Violet looked as if
she was itching to sew him some curtains
on the spot.

"Yeah, Mom, you've got great taste,"
Chase said as he looked in the cupboards
for plates.

"Thanks, kiddo. You're being so sweet
to me. Giving me compliments. Inviting me for pizza. What happened to my
child?" she asked, pretending to look
around.

"Mom, I'm right here," Chase said, rolling his eyes.

Violet leaned down and pressed a kiss
on his cheek. Deacon loved watching
the interplay between mother and son.
The love they felt for one another was
effusive. He prayed that one day he and
Chase would share a bond this powerful. *In time,* he reminded himself. Strong

294   *His Secret Alaskan Family*

relationships weren't built in an instant. He just needed to be patient and lay the bricks for the foundation.

Over cheese and pepperoni pizza, they listened as Chase cracked jokes and regaled them with Maverick's latest hijinks. Seeing Violet laugh so uproariously gave him such a contented feeling, one that settled deep down in his soul. This dinner reminded Deacon that if things had worked out differently, this would be his reality all the time. Family suppers with Violet and Chase. Laughter and stories. Joy and connectivity.

When they went to check on Chase, he was curled up in a ball. Deacon's chest tightened at the sight of his son resting so peacefully. How many moments like this had he missed out on in Chase's life? There were so many phases he hadn't been a part of—Chase as a newborn, the toddler years, all the way up till now.

"He used to look just like that as a baby

in his crib," Violet said, reaching out and stroking his hair. She looked over at Deacon. "I'm sorry you missed out on those years. It's not fair."

His throat felt constricted as he said, "Thanks for saying so. One of these days, I'd love to see your photos. First steps. Birthdays. School photos. That would mean a lot to me."

She made a tutting sound. "I'm sorry that I didn't think of that. It's just been such a whirlwind since you came back. But I have plenty of albums all featuring Chase."

"It's okay. I know my coming back was unexpected, to say the least." He placed a comfy throw over Chase, then put a finger to his lips. "He'll be okay tonight sleeping here if it's okay with you."

"Of course it is. He looks tuckered out," she whispered. "There's no sense in waking him up. I'm going to head out."

Deacon trailed behind her as she headed

toward the front door and put on her jacket. He couldn't really explain why, but the thought of her leaving caused a sense of longing to rise up inside of him. What would it be like, he wondered, to truly be a family with Violet? No separate houses. No co-parenting. Just togetherness.

A part of him knew it was foolish to dream about things that wouldn't come to pass. He simply had to accept that this chapter of his life would be centered on becoming the best father he could be. And that would have to be enough.

"This was nice," she said. "Thanks for making Chase so happy."

"That's pretty much what I live for these days," he admitted. "If he's content then all is right with my world."

"You're a quick study," she said, smiling. "Fatherhood suits you."

"Can I walk you home?" he asked. Honestly, he was eager to spend as much time in her presence as possible. The vibe between them this evening had been heart-warming.

"That's a kind offer, but I'll be fine. You should stay here with Chase in case he wakes up."

"All right then. I'll bring him home in the morning."

Before he was truly ready to say good-bye, Violet headed off down the path toward the Drummond property. He stood by the front door as long as he could, watching her until she disappeared into the night.

Sticking around Serenity Peak hadn't been part of the plan when he had first arrived in town. He'd wanted to establish a relationship with Chase before he went back to Chicago and to try to make up for all the lost years. And now he felt conflicted about his plans. His feelings for Violet were intensifying by the moment. Just now he had been tempted to take her in his arms and kiss her.

But that wasn't what Violet wanted.

She'd made things quite clear. They were firmly in the friend zone, even though he yearned to be much more to her.

Chapter Fourteen

❧

Violet couldn't ask for better weather. The sun was shining, and the temperature was mild enough to switch up her winter parka for a lightweight jacket. She couldn't remember the last time the sky had been such a perfect shade of blue. She wished that her mind was as peaceful as this Alaskan weather.

A fun outing with Autumn would serve as a great distraction from everything she had been preoccupied about. The kiss she'd shared with Deacon, the incident at the Midnight Sun spring festival and her growing feelings for her ex-fiancé were all swirling around in her mind. Everything in her life seemed chaotic. Where had her orderly life gone?

Pizza at his place had been wonderful, but what did it mean? Where did things stand between them? Was it merely friendship? If so, why was she still dreaming about the tender kiss they had shared?

Her phone pinged as a text from Autumn arrived.

I'm here. Grabbed a table for us by the window.

Once she entered the Humbled coffee shop, she quickly greeted Molly, the owner of the place and Skye's best friend. She couldn't be happier for Molly, who'd merged her love of books and coffee via the café bookstore.

Violet looked around the establishment, easily spotting Autumn's cranberry-colored jacket and matching beret. As she had indicated, Autumn was sitting in a sunny spot by a window. Violet rushed over and sank down into the chair across from her friend. "Sorry I'm late. Things have been so hectic lately that I rarely know if I'm coming or going." She exhaled a deep breath.

"Let me go place our orders with Molly so you can sit back and relax. Your usual?" Autumn asked. Violet nodded her head. It was a blessing to have a dear friend who knew her regular order and went out of her way to take care of her.

Five minutes later and Autumn was back with two chai lattes and chocolate croissants. Violet's mood lifted as soon as she laid eyes on the treats.

"Oh, bless you," she said, raising the drink to her lips and taking a lengthy sip.

"I thought you would be able to relax more now that Deacon is assuming his parental role with Chase. How's that working out?" Autumn asked.

A huge lump sat in her throat. Rather

than try to get the words out, Violet shrugged.

"Talk to me, Violet. I've laid a lot of my issues on your shoulders. For once, you can lean on me. That's what friends do."

"I know, Autumn. Honestly, I've really gotten in my head about Deacon. Our past. The present. It's gotten a bit confusing. Lines are getting a bit blurred."

"That's perfectly understandable. You were engaged and planning a life together." She bit into her croissant. "You can't pretend as if that never happened."

"Exactly. And he's different now. So am I. But that doesn't mean our connection has been severed. Honestly, sometimes it feels that we're more bonded than ever."

"I didn't tell you this before, but he and I had a little chat when he first came to town," Autumn said. "We crossed paths at Northern Lights."

"What did you chat about?" Violet asked, her curiosity piqued.

"You, of course. I made it clear that he

needed to tread lightly with you." She made a fierce face. "Or else he would have to deal with me. I have to admit that he really seems to care about you and Chase. That's a good sign."

Although hearing this information from her best friend was reassuring, she had no indication from Deacon that she was anything more than the mother of his child. One kiss wasn't exactly a declaration of love. Being in this limbo left her open and vulnerable in a way she'd vowed never to be again. She wasn't sure she could withstand any more heartache.

"I don't want to complain because Chase has always wanted a father, and it's turned out to be such a tremendous blessing. I never imagined that Deacon would come back to Serenity Peak. I truly believed that I would never see him again."

"You're handling things really well if you ask me," Autumn said. "I mean, talk about a shock to the system. It kind of makes when I came back divorced and pregnant pale in comparison," she said, giggling.

Violet laughed along with her. At the time, it hadn't been so funny since both Judah and Autumn had been at a crossroads in their lives.

"Honestly, I thought that I had my life all figured out after years of struggling to move past him." She let out a ragged breath. "We were doing fine, Chase and I. Just fine. But then Deacon came back to Serenity Peak without the slightest warning."

"Rude!" Autumn said with a smirk.

"And it's not fair that he's only gotten more handsome with age," Violet grumbled. "Tall, dark and handsome for days."

Autumn studied her from across the table.

"You're in love with him, aren't you?" Autumn asked. A knowing look was stamped on her face. "It's written all over your face."

"Yes, I am. It's as if my heart woke

up the moment he came back to Serenity Peak." A brittle laugh slipped past her lips. "I don't think I truly ever stopped loving him," she admitted. "In order to survive my broken heart, I tucked all those feelings aside and made myself move on."

"But now he's back, which means you two have a shot at getting things right this time around," Autumn said.

"But how do I trust that this time things will be different?" she asked, letting out a sob. "I don't want to get my heart broken all over again."

Autumn patted her hand. "I know how you feel, Violet. I went through something similar with Judah. In my opinion, love is stepping out on a limb of faith and believing in something that's not always crystal clear."

"But what if he doesn't stick around? I keep thinking he's going to up and leave us. Maybe head back to his family in Chicago."

"You're thinking because he left once before he'll do it again. Am I right?" Autumn asked. "Maybe you should tell him how you feel," Autumn suggested.

She shook her head. "I'm too chicken. You're so much braver than I am when it comes to matters of the heart."

"No risk, no reward," Autumn crowed. "That's what my dad always told us."

Violet picked at her croissant. "What if he doesn't feel the same way? That would be so awkward."

"Well, he kissed you, didn't he?" Autumn asked in a loud voice that garnered her attention from a few other patrons.

"Shhh," Violet said. "The last thing we need is more gossip."

"Sorry," Autumn said, lowering her voice. "But you did share a kiss, so there's that. He isn't indifferent to you."

"Well he's certainly not going out of his way to tell me how he feels," Violet said, feeling a bit downcast. A kiss was one thing. Things would be so different if Deacon let her know how he felt. Then she wouldn't feel so up in the air with her own feelings.

Something had to give. One way or another, she needed to let Deacon know how she felt…or find a way to deal with the fact that they were going to be just friends and co-parents.

Lord, give me the strength to be courageous. Allow me to accept that certain things are out of my control. Let me face the future with grace.

If anyone had told Deacon a year ago that he would be picking up his son from an afterschool program, he wouldn't have believed it. In the short time that he'd been back in Serenity Peak, Chase had become such an important part of his life, so much so that he sometimes forgot their relationship was brand new.

At four o'clock sharp, a bunch of kids exited the small school building. Deacon craned his neck searching for Chase in the crowd. After all the other students had departed, he finally saw Chase come outside, accompanied by a woman he assumed to be one of his teachers. She was petite, with salt-and-pepper hair. He couldn't read her expression, but Chase looked put out. As he drew closer, Deacon noticed swelling by one of his eyes.

Deacon vaulted from the truck and met them halfway.

"What happened to your eye?" he asked Chase. Instead of answering, Chase looked down at the ground. Deacon looked over at Chase's teacher.

"Hello, I'm Coretta O'Grady, one of the afterschool teachers. You're Deacon's father. Am I correct?" the woman asked.

"Yes, I'm Deacon Shaw," he said, extending his hand. "It's a pleasure to meet you."

"Unfortunately, Chase got into a scuffle with a fellow student. I broke it up immediately, but both boys are going to miss a day of school as punishment."

Deacon swung his gaze to Chase, who was studiously ignoring him. "Chase, have you apologized yet?"

"I'm sorry, Mrs. O'Grady," he mumbled. He briefly looked up at her then back down at the ground.

"Chase, go get in the truck," Deacon said, annoyed at his son's lack of contrition. His eye was swelling up by the second, and he couldn't imagine what Violet would say about the situation.

Once Chase was out of earshot, Deacon pressed for more information. "Any idea of what caused the fight?" He had a bad feeling that this was spillover from the festival. He prayed that he wasn't at the center of this mess.

"I couldn't find that out, but I will say that lately Chase hasn't been himself. I can't recall a single instance of him ever fighting with another student or even raising his voice. It's just so unlike him. Normally, he's everyone's buddy."

Deacon experienced a sinking sensation

in the pit of his stomach. *Lately Chase hasn't been himself.* The only thing that had changed as of late was his arrival in town and his presence in his son's life.

"I'm so sorry for the trouble," Deacon apologized. "This won't happen again."

He strode over to the truck and jumped inside. Chase was looking down at his hands and not at him. "Are you mad at me?" Chase asked in a soft voice.

"Just disappointed and a bit confused," Deacon admitted. "Where is all of this coming from? I thought things were good at school."

"It is," Chase insisted. "But if someone is talking about my family, I'm not going to ignore it." His expression was mutinous. "Ethan was running his mouth."

Ethan. The same boy from the day of the Midnight Sun spring festival. Clearly, their issue hadn't been resolved.

"Are you familiar with Matthew 5:39? The verse about turning the other cheek?"

Deacon asked. "Something tells me you are."

"Yes, but it's hard to remember things like that in the heat of the moment," Chase explained, his hazel eyes huge in his face.

"That's the important thing about living in our faith. We need to hold strong, especially during stressful times. It's what I've tried to do when the worst things imaginable were happening in my life."

"I'm sorry," Chase said, a tear sliding down his cheek. As he wiped the moisture away, Chase winced. "Ouch," he said. "My eye is starting to hurt."

"We need to get you home and put a bag of frozen peas on that eye. It's not looking too good at the moment. You're going to have a shiner by the morning."

Chase grinned at him. "That's okay, Dad. I didn't get the worst of it."

Deacon let out a groan. "Chase. In your own words, say less."

When they reached the Drummonds'

home, Chase appeared reluctant to get out of the truck. Deacon knew he was dreading Violet seeing his puffy eye, which was now darkening into a full-fledged black eye.

"Come on," he said, gesturing for his son to exit the truck. "Time to face the music."

Once they were inside, it wasn't long before Violet came looking for Chase. She let out a shocked squeal the moment she saw him.

"Chase!" she exclaimed. "What in the world happened to you?"

Chase looked over at Deacon with a pleading expression. "Can you tell her?"

Deacon shook his head. "No, son. Your mother needs to hear an explanation from you. I wasn't there when the trouble broke out."

Chase hung his head. "I got into a fight."

Violet let out a shocked sound. "A fight? With who? Over what?" she asked, throwing out one question after the other.

"I don't tolerate physical violence. What's gotten into you, Chase?"

"Ethan. He was talking about my dad, okay? I was telling everyone that my dad was a hero, and he said that he wasn't." Chase's cheeks reddened. He clenched his fists at his side. "And I know you want me to feel bad about what I did, but I don't."

Deacon felt sick hearing Chase defending his reputation like this. It was the last thing he wanted to happen. Chase shouldn't be placed in this awful situation. But there was literally nothing he could do about it. And his son was suffering because of him.

Violet threw her hands in the air. "I know your instinct was to protect your father's reputation, but he doesn't want you to take this on. He's capable of dealing with this situation himself."

Chase folded his arms across his chest. "I got suspended too, but just for a day," he added, holding up his hands. Violet shook her head, not bothering to hide her disappointment.

"Let's put something on that eye," Violet said, her tone softening. She opened up the freezer and rummaged around inside. She turned toward Chase and said, "This might sting," before placing a bag of frozen peas underneath his eye.

"Ow," Chase said, flinching at the contact. "It really hurts."

"Let that be a lesson," Violet chided. "Flying fists is never a good idea."

"The frozen peas are a necessary evil," Deacon said. "Trust me, it'll help the swelling go down."

"Did you have black eyes as a kid?" Chase asked. He was watching Deacon like a hawk with his good eye, awaiting his answer.

Deacon wasn't sure Violet would appreciate the truth in this case. Chase might take his answer as encouragement, which was the last thing he wanted. "I plead the Fifth," he said, skirting the issue. He felt an ache in his chest over this situation that wouldn't subside. He wanted to be a role model for his son, not a disruption to his orderly life.

A few minutes later, Chase was in his room writing a letter of apology to Mrs. O'Grady. Deacon was pacing back and forth while Violet was muttering about what type of punishment Chase should receive. It was clear to Deacon that this was all his fault. He hadn't prepared Chase for this type of scenario. He hadn't wanted to believe that the towns-folk would put his family through this. He'd truly believed that life in Serenity Peak would be as idyllic as it had been in the past.

But here he was, feeling incredibly jaded and sick at heart. A sense of frustration threatened to choke him. If he wasn't able to be a positive force for Chase, then what was the point? He didn't want his son to fight his battles.

Violet was looking at him with concern. "Deacon, why don't you sit down. You're going to wear a hole in the floor at this rate."

He sank into a chair and ran a hand over his face. "I don't belong here. Maybe the truth is that I don't belong anywhere."

"What do you mean by that?" she asked. "This situation is concerning, but you're taking it too personally."

"How can I not?" he asked. "This is about me. And my past. My reputation in this town."

Violet sat down next to him. "I thought we told Chase not to let town gossip bring him down. But here you are getting consumed by it."

"Obviously, Chase isn't listening to our advice. He got into another scuffle. He has a black eye and a suspension." He shoved his hands into his front pockets. "This isn't right. His whole life is in a tailspin because of me."

She placed her hand on his arm. "You need to calm down. Unfortunately, kids do get into fights. It's not a good thing, but it's also not a reason to ring alarm bells."

Alarm bells were definitely sounding off in his head. What had started out to be a joyful homecoming was now a major disruption for Chase. He couldn't simply sit back and let Chase's life fall apart.

He splayed his hands on the table. "I'm just not sure if staying here in Serenity Peak is the right decision. Going back to Chicago might be the best move for all of us."

She let out a shocked sound. "You can't be serious!"

"I am," Deacon said. "I wouldn't joke about this. What's the point of being here if it's going to hurt our son?"

"You'll break Chase's heart!" Violet cried out.

Deacon knew Chase would be upset, but eventually things would go back to the way they'd been before his unexpected arrival in town. The rumors would die down, and Chase wouldn't be in upheaval. He wouldn't disappear from his son's life. They could write letters or exchange emails outside of prying eyes.

"You were getting along just fine before I came back. And my staying here wasn't supposed to be long-term anyway." But he'd fallen in love with his son. And Violet. Those feelings had made him believe that remaining in Serenity Peak was the right move.

Violet appeared stricken. "We might have looked like that on the surface, but the truth is that Chase had a big void in his life." Her voice cracked. "You've managed to fill that hole. He needed a father, Deacon. He needed you. *Needs* you. And you delivered."

Although a part of him was listening to what Violet was saying, another part of him rejected her words.

"I wish that I could believe that, because it feels as if I'm just playing catch up," he said, abruptly getting to his feet.

"Violet, I've spent so many years not having any choices about my life when I was on the run, but now I do." He deeply inhaled. "When I came back, it was only supposed to be a brief stay so I could explain things to you. My plan was always to head back to Chicago and be with my dad. I wanted to help him out with the business." He let out a groan. "And I've probably confused Chase by going back and forth about it, making him feel uncertain about my presence in his life." He raked his hand through his hair. "The truth is, I still haven't decided whether to stay put or head back to Chicago."

Chapter Fifteen

Pain speared through Violet's midsection as she watched Deacon tear out of the house and race away in his truck. What had just happened? Deacon had become completely undone by Chase's fight and his belief that he'd played a role in the situation. And his proposed solution to the escalating situation was to leave Serenity Peak? Was he so used to being on the run that it had become his default move?

Didn't he know what that would do to Chase? And to her. She had ached to tell him that she was in love with him, but fear held her back. If he intended to leave her again, he couldn't possibly love her. Leaving last time had been one thing. He'd been justified by the possibility of danger back then. Now, his decision would be a choice—and people didn't choose to leave the ones they loved. Or at least they shouldn't.

Losing Deacon a second time would be just as painful as the first. And not only would her heart be broken, but Chase would be shattered by Deacon's departure too. To be fair, Deacon's original plan hadn't involved sticking around in Serenity Peak, but with each passing day, she was clinging to the idea of his stay becoming permanent. They needed him in their lives.

But how pathetic would it look for her to beg him to stay and profess her love in the process? That might come across as manipulative.

This almost felt like a déjà vu moment. She had fallen apart like this ten years ago when he had packed up and left town. What if this time she never saw him again?

Tears ran down her face as she thought about all the good things Deacon had brought into their lives. He had been a godsend at Sugar Works, coming to the rescue when they'd been dealing with the infestation of the birch trees. He had shown Chase nothing but love and fatherly devotion. And somehow, without even realizing it, she'd started to lean on him as someone important to her life. Everything was better with Deacon around. His loyalty and compassion were testaments to his character. After all he had been through, Deacon still invested in others. He continued to make forward strides.

They were just some of the many reasons why she loved him.

It was strange how for all these years she had been putting one foot in front of the other without realizing that half of her heart was missing. Or maybe she had known all along but swept those feelings under the rug to avoid the pain.

"Mom." Chase's voice called to her from the entryway. "Are you crying because of me? What I did?"

She swiped away her tears as she always did. This time it was too late to prevent Chase from seeing. "No, Chase, I'm just sad because Deacon is really upset about all the gossip. He blames himself."

Chase quirked his mouth. "It's not his fault that some people can't stop flapping their gums."

Violet felt a little smile tugging at her lips. This was the beauty of kids, she thought. A person could be down, and all it took was a phrase like that to lighten the mood. Chase was Deacon's defender, and it showed just how close they had become in only a short period.

"I couldn't have said it any better myself." Pride burst inside her chest. Despite the trouble at school, he was a good kid, caring and loving. He had a moral compass and a sense of compassion for those around him. He was the best of both her and Deacon. Raising him as a single mother in a small town hadn't been easy, but in moments like this one, Violet knew she'd done something right.

"So does that mean I'm not going to be punished?" Chase asked, crossing his hands prayerfully in front of him.

"That would be an incorrect assumption. Bad behavior still warrants consequences," Violet said as her son let out a loud groan.

He shrugged. "It was worth a try."

"Listen. I need to tell you something. Your dad has been through a lot, Chase. He's struggled. He's lost so much through the years. His mother died while he was in witness protection. Your grandmother." Just the thought of Deacon not being able to say goodbye to his mother choked her up. "That's a tremendous loss. Not to mention he missed nine years of your life. All of this has taken a big toll on him."

Chase's eyes moistened. "I feel bad about that. It doesn't seem fair."

"That's not why I told you. It's just that I want you to be able to understand why he might be very upset about the rumors and your situation at school. I suspect it's hard for your dad not to blame himself. He's used to carrying a lot of guilt on his shoulders." She wasn't going to upset Chase by telling him that Deacon had just mentioned he might leave town. If that happened, and she prayed it didn't, Chase would be inconsolable. His entire world would be turned upside down.

"We should do something. Gramps always says that if we want to make a difference, we need to act. That means we can't just let people get away with spreading lies."

Chase's voice sounded strong and sure. Her baby was growing up and wanting to take a stand against things that went against his personal code of conduct. And he was right. They couldn't sit on the sidelines and do nothing, say nothing. They were a family, and these rumors were affecting all of them.

She stood up and embraced him. "Chase, I'm super proud to be your mom. I don't like you scrapping with your classmates, but I love just everything else about you. And you're right. We can't allow this to continue."

Chase rubbed his hands together. "So what's the plan, Mom?"

Just then, Abel walked into the room. "I couldn't help but overhear the two of you. Consider me on board with operation rumor control. I want to do my part to end this nonsense. I was born and bred in this town, and I refuse to allow a few bad apples to ruin this community."

"That's right, Dad," Violet said, speaking past the raw emotion. She was now crying happy tears. Her father never let her down, even in her darkest moments.

When she had told him about being pregnant with Chase, his only concern had been her having a healthy baby.

Chase pumped his fist in the air. "All right, Gramps. Let's do this."

Violet looked back and forth between her father and Chase with a heart overflowing with love. She wasn't alone in this, not by a long shot. And neither was Deacon. They just needed him to realize that he was so very loved and worthy of a second chance in Serenity Peak.

Deacon inhaled the pristine air and surveyed the view from the Halcyon Mountains. Mere words couldn't describe the most breathtaking views he'd ever seen in Alaska. The hiking trails had provided a hearty workout that released plenty of endorphins. For the first time in a long time, he felt at peace. Sean had invited him here for a hike, knowing that he had a lot weighing on his heart and mind. His friend clearly knew the healing powers of this amazing location.

The weather was perfect, with only a slight chill to remind them that they were in Alaska. The snow on the peaks was beginning to melt. It was amazing, he thought, what a tranquil vista could do for one's outlook.

On the way up the mountain, they paused for a water break, sitting on a rock ledge that provided stunning views of Kachemak Bay and most of Serenity Peak.

"This has got to be the closest thing to paradise on earth," Sean said as he surveyed the beautiful Alaskan landscape.

"Thanks for the invite," Deacon said. "It's just what I needed to decompress."

"So, what's up?" Sean asked. "You said there was something going on. Is this about Chase's black eye?"

"You heard about that?" Deacon asked, stunned at how fast things got around in small towns.

Sean rolled his eyes. "I own a popular

establishment. People talk. But honestly, it wasn't anything nasty. Everyone adores Chase."

Deacon let out a breath of relief. "That's good to know. I… I'm thinking of leaving town." He deliberately didn't look over at his friend, knowing he would be shocked and disappointed.

Sure enough, Sean let out a gasp. "Seriously? So soon? I thought you were going to stick around for a while."

"Yeah, that was the plan, until the gossip mill went into overdrive. I can't seem to convince folks that I'm a decent guy. And it's hurting Chase, which in turn harms Violet," Deacon explained. "I can't allow that to happen, not after everything she's been through."

"Is it that serious, though, to warrant you leaving Serenity Peak? And what about your son?" Sean asked. "That's going to be agonizing for you both."

"Chase's life was on an even keel before I arrived here. Now he's gotten in two fights, has a black eye and a school suspension, all because he was trying to defend me against town gossip." He took a swig from his water bottle. "He's a kid. That shouldn't be his responsibility. He's carrying around adult-size burdens."

Sean shook his head. "He's a loyal kid who loves his dad. That's a good thing."

"And I love him too, which is why it's killing me to see him being placed in this position." Deacon tried to block out the little voice that was telling him leaving was wrong. "If I'm gone, the rumors will die down."

"But what about Chase? He loses the father he finally has in his life? That doesn't seem very fair. Have you thought about how that's going to affect him?"

Deacon met Sean's gaze. His friend looked flabbergasted. Maybe he hadn't thought this through.

"It's not that I want to leave," he said. "I want to protect Chase. Isn't that what fatherhood is all about?"

"Deacon, I'm talking to you as a friend, so I hope you'll hear me out. I think you've gotten used to being on the run over the years. You've become a little de-sensitized to it." He held up his hands as Deacon opened his mouth to rebut him. "I understand that you were forced into going from place to place, hiding your true identity. You didn't have a choice! But maybe a part of you has been condi-tioned to run when things go wrong. It's become an instinct."

He opened his mouth to respond, but no words came out.

"You've been a fighter all these years, Deacon. That's how you made it through your trials and tribulations. Why don't you stick around and fight now? For Chase. And for Violet. For the life you deserve."

"Violet?" he asked, furrowing his brows.

Sean sent him a knowing look. "You still love her. I can hear it in your voice every time you say her name. Just admit it."

Deacon let out the breath he'd been

holding. "Is it that obvious?" he asked. So far, he'd thought that he had done a pretty good job of hiding it.

Sean nodded and said, "Probably not to everyone, but anyone who truly knows you will figure it out."

"Loving her is the easiest thing I've ever done," he admitted. "When I came back to Alaska, I honestly thought those feelings had been packed away, but I was wrong. Before I knew it, she was right there under my skin. I don't think those feelings ever truly went away."

"The kind of love you and Violet shared was pretty epic. I'm not surprised feelings like that are still knocking around."

"I'm pretty sure they're one-sided," Deacon told him. Unrequited love didn't feel very good. He was pining away for the only woman he'd ever truly loved.

"What makes you think that?" Sean asked.

"We shared a kiss, and then she said it was a mistake" he admitted. He placed his hand over his heart. "Which was like a dagger in my chest. Ouch."

"But she kissed you back?" Sean asked.

"Yes," he said, his mind replaying the kiss. He had relived the moment dozens of times in his head. Every instinct told him that she'd enjoyed it just as much as he had. "Honestly, now that I think about it, maybe she was overwhelmed by everything going on."

"You think?" Sean asked. "Not only did her ex-fiancé show up in town after a decade-long absence, but she had to introduce you to the son you never knew about. Plus, she's had Chase to worry about as well as the diseased trees at Sugar Works. All while juggling work and a nine-year-old. Throw in some ugly rumors, and you have yourself one stressed-out lady."

All this time, he had been denying what he felt radiating from Violet. He'd told himself it was just wishful thinking, but it did feel very similar to how things had been between them in the past. Of course, there were present-day obstacles, but there wasn't anything they couldn't conquer. He'd made it through the worst and emerged in one piece.

"You're right. I can't throw it all away, Sean. Most of all, I can't show Chase that running away is the answer. I'm supposed to be a role model." If he walked away from Chase now, it could be disastrous for their relationship, as Violet had suggested. And it would be cowardly to leave everything on Violet's plate. He didn't want the woman he loved to have to pick up all the pieces of a mess he'd created.

Sean raised an eyebrow. "And Violet? What are you going to do about her?"

He clenched his teeth. "I'm going to fight, Sean. Not just for Chase, but for Violet as well. Like you said, I'm not a quitter."

"That's right," Sean said, letting out a rallying cry from his football glory days.

Deacon chuckled. Hope blossomed inside of him. It was amazing how twenty-four hours could change one's perspective. The passage from Psalm 30:5 swept over him, the same one that had always been his mother's favorite. *Weeping may endure for a night, but joy cometh in the morning.*

Chapter Sixteen

Sunday morning dawned bright and beautiful. Violet woke with a feeling of conviction flowing through her veins. Although she hadn't seen Deacon or spoken to him in a few days, she felt certain that he would show up this morning for Sunday service at Serenity Church. Especially since Chase had asked him to come to support his class's bake sale in the church basement.

Not only would a large group be present at church, but the gathering afterward was always standing room only. Free food from Northern Lights and other restaurants was a huge inducement to attend. With the children hosting a bake sale, attendance would be high. Violet had racked her brain to come up with a location where she could reach as many townsfolk as possible at one time. This one made the most sense.

She got on her knees beside her bed and prayed. For courage. And favor. She bowed her head and crossed her hands.

Lord, let us win over hearts and minds today. Grant us favor.

Violet headed downstairs to the kitchen, pressing a kiss on her father's cheek as he sat drinking his morning coffee. She made some oatmeal and eggs for Chase to tide him over until after the service. He didn't need a full breakfast since they would be eating in the hall after church, but by that time he would be ravenous.

"Is Deacon coming over here to go to service with us?" she asked. Her nerves were beginning to fray. At some point,

338 His Secret Alaskan Family

she needed to make a plea to Deacon to stay in town. If necessary, she would swallow her pride and let him know that she loved him.

"Dad said he's going to meet us at church," Chase said, speaking past a mouthful of oatmeal. "He had an errand to run, I think."

Her stomach dipped with disappointment. She ached to see Deacon's face, to look into his eyes and make sure that he hadn't left town. Although a part of her knew he wouldn't take off without saying goodbye, another part of her fretted over losing him. She knew these were leftover feelings from the past and the lingering sense of loss from ten years ago.

Dragging herself out of her thoughts, she focused on Chase. "Okay, you better go and get dressed for church," Violet advised him. "We need to leave in half an hour."

"I am dressed," he said, looking down at his T-shirt and flannel pants.

Her father let out a throaty laugh. "That's what you think!"

"You can do better than that. Those are your pajamas," Violet said, trying not to laugh out loud. "How about the blue oxford shirt and a pair of cords?"

"Okay," Chase said. "I can live with that." He got up from the table, placed his bowl in the sink and headed upstairs to get dressed.

"How you feeling?" Abel asked.

"A little nervous, but I know I'm in the right. Something needs to be said," Violet told him. "I appreciate all the support. Ryan, Skye and Lula will be there too, as well as Autumn and Judah."

"Well, that's good. Judah and Ryan know firsthand about what gossip can do to people. The way certain folks gossiped about Judah's wife after the accident was horrible. And it drove Judah and his brother Leif apart."

That had been a terrible situation. Mary

Campbell had died along with her son, Zane, in a horrific car accident on a rainy night. In the aftermath, cruel whispers had spread about Mary being under the influence at the time of the crash. Nothing could have been further from the truth, yet the gossip still spread, causing pain in the process.

It was high time this issue was nipped in the bud. If she had to get the conversation going, so be it. She wanted to show Chase that he had a mother who would fight for what was just and good. Sitting on the sidelines and watching her family get hurt didn't sit well with her.

By the time they arrived at Serenity Church, the congregation had almost filled all of the pews. Violet discreetly looked around for Deacon, but she didn't see him anywhere. She found a seat in the front for the three of them, figuring they could scoot over when Deacon arrived. Skye waved to her from another row as she held Lula in her arms and swayed to the opening hymn. Ryan was by her side, singing along with his hymnal in hand.

The service was beautiful, with uplifting music and a strong sermon. Violet wondered if something was in the air since gossip was the subject. Maybe she and her family weren't the only ones who were sick and tired of lies being spread. When the service ended, the congregation dispersed and everyone headed downstairs for fellowship and food. Chase ran off to look for Deacon in the crowd as Violet chatted amiably with some of the parishioners and a few friends.

"Go ahead, Violet. Don't lose your nerve. I've got your back," Abel said, nudging her forward when there was a lull in the conversation. There was a small stage with a podium and a microphone mere feet away.

She didn't know where Deacon and Chase were, but this was her moment to speak out on Deacon's behalf. If she waited any longer, the crowd might thin out.

Taking a fortifying breath, she headed toward the podium and grabbed the mic. She flicked its power switch and tapped it to make sure it was working. Then she began to speak. "Hello, everyone. I hope you're enjoying this beautiful Sunday service. Most of you know me. I'm Violet Drummond, Abel's daughter and Chase's mom. Skye's big sister. I've lived in Serenity Peak all of my life, and this is the only church community I've ever known." People in the crowd nodded as she spoke, while some called out to her by name. Autumn and Judah made their way to the front of the crowd, giving her strength with their presence. "The reason I'm speaking today is on behalf of my son and his father, Deacon Shaw."

Whispers rippled through the crowd. Some of the expressions were shocked, while others were encouraging. The sight of Chase standing with Abel was just the impetus she needed.

Fear not, for I am with you.

"He's a good man," she continued. "No, let me correct myself. He's a great man. And an amazing father. That's a good place for me to start. No matter what, he's part of the Drummond family, and he's welcome here in Serenity Peak."

Skye, Ryan, Lula and her father were standing nearby. Skye flashed her a thumbs-up sign.

"This town needs to stop tearing people down. The whispers. The ugly gossip. Truth doesn't seem to be important anymore." She was trembling with outrage. "This isn't the first time, but I pray it will be the last." She drew herself up to her full height. "In case you're interested in facts, Deacon was in the Witness Protection Program after witnessing a terrible crime. He risked his own safety to become a federal witness and help put the criminals responsible behind bars. And then when he was the target of their revenge, he did the only thing he could do. He entered witness protection, leaving everything he knew behind."

She looked around the room at the startled expressions. Clearly, most of the townsfolk had no idea of Deacon's backstory. "Can you imagine how difficult his journey has been, moving from place to place when the danger became too insurmountable? How much he's suffered? And now when he's finally free and embracing the son he just found out about, this rumor mongering is hanging over his head like a dark cloud. Frankly, all of the gossips should be ashamed of themselves."

Abel stepped forward, speaking in a commanding voice that didn't need a microphone. "What Violet is saying in a nutshell is that this needs to stop. Gossip like this ruins lives. This type of behavior needs to be cut out because it's cancerous to a community like ours." He spread his arms wide. "Just ask Judah or Ryan. They went through something similar."

"It almost tore my family apart," Judah said, cradling his son, River, in his arms.

"It nearly broke us," Ryan added. He leaned in closer and put an arm around Skye.

"We've got to do better as a community," Skye said. "If we hear ugly rumors, we need to shut them down. Fires are snuffed out without oxygen."

"Hear! Hear!" Dr. Poppy called out, clapping vigorously. She was a no-nonsense physician who was well respected in town. Gideon and Sadie were clapping louder than anyone.

The sentiment spread, with the majority of the crowd breaking into applause and vowing to shut down the rumor mill. Violet didn't think she had ever seen the community so worked up about anything. As the townsfolk dug into the food, she was deluged with words of praise from the congregation. The general consensus was that she was brave for confronting evil in their community.

Chase ran over and wrapped his arms around her. "You did good, Mom. Dad thinks so too." Hearing words of praise from her son made her feel like a superhero.

"Thanks, buddy," she said, hugging him back. "Doing what's right always feels good. Try and remember that."

Violet looked across the room and spotted Deacon surrounded by well-wishers. People were shaking his hand and welcoming him to Serenity Peak in the manner they should have when he'd first arrived. This, she thought, was the town community she'd always loved. There was so much good in this room and in her beloved hometown. She prayed Deacon could feel it as well and that he'd changed his mind about leaving.

Emotions were riding high, and suddenly it seemed as if the walls were closing in on her. The hall was packed to capacity, so much so that she was finding it hard to breathe.

"I'll be right back. I need some fresh air," she said to Chase, quickly rushing toward the back door and making her way outside.

Once the cool air hit her face, Violet drew in some deep breaths. She immediately felt better. So much was still weighing on her, and it all seemed to hinge on Deacon's decision. Was he going to stay in town? She had done everything possible to make his decision easier. Even if he stayed but they were never together again as a couple, she could accept that. But she couldn't bear the thought of him walking away again.

Please, Lord. Don't make me go through losing Deacon all over again. I'm not sure that I can bear such a tremendous loss.

Deacon had rarely felt as touched by a gesture in his life as he did at this moment. For a man who tended to keep his emotions in check, he was now as wide open as the Alaskan tundra.

Hearing Violet vigorously defend him had been a powerful moment, not to mention an emotional one. She had blown him away with her willingness to speak on his behalf to the townsfolk! It had taken grit and courage to talk from the heart like that. But, as he'd always known, she was a woman of impeccable strength and character.

That was one of the main reasons he loved her so dearly.

"Violet." Deacon choked out her name as he walked toward her. He'd watched her rush outside the fellowship hall and then followed her. She turned to face him, her eyes bright with emotion.

"Deacon. I was looking all over for you," she said, sounding relieved.

"The church was crowded when I came in, so I had to sit in the back. I was just with Chase in the hall, so he knows I'm here to support his bake sale." He planned to support Chase in all his endeavors, big and small. He was keenly aware that he was making up for lost time.

"I know he appreciates your support," Violet said. "You mean the world to him."

It didn't matter how many times Violet said those words to him. They always lifted him up to the stratosphere. Being Chase's dad was everything!

"What you said back there...it was amazing. I've never had anyone in my life speak on my behalf like that," Deacon told her. "It means all the more because it came from you."

"I only spoke the truth," Violet said. "And it was high time someone confronted them. Sadly, this kind of stuff has been going on for years. Judah and his brother were estranged because of town gossip. And when baby Lula was dropped off at Sugar's Place, rumors were rampant all over town. It's all so unnecessary."

"I'm sorry I let the rumors get to me.

All I could think was that I was going to be a detriment to our son." He gritted his teeth. "I only want good things for Chase, and the thought of getting in the way of that gutted me. I've caused so much pain to so many people, and our son is the last person I want to cause harm to."

"Oh no, that's not true, Deacon. He's proud of you." She took a step closer toward him so that there were only inches between them. "As he should be. Please don't leave us."

Us. The word gave him hope. If she wanted him to stay in Serenity Peak because of her, then he was able to hope as he'd done before.

He held her face between his hands. "I'm not going anywhere, Violet. This town can't get rid of me that easily," he said with a chuckle.

She closed her eyes for a moment then opened them. "Oh, that is such a relief. I've been so worried about history repeating itself."

"That's not happening. Chase is here. You're here," he said tenderly. "There's no other place I'd rather be."

"Music to my ears," Violet said. "I can't tell you what it means to my family to have you working with us at Sugar Works."

"Yet another reason for staying put. You've made me feel like I'm valued there. I've always felt that I belonged here in Serenity Peak, but I knew all those years ago, that I wasn't on solid ground to make a life here." He placed a kiss on her forehead. "All that has changed, my love. I want you and Chase to be at the center of my new life here."

"You do?" she asked, her eyes radiating surprise.

"Yes, I do. I love you, Violet. I've loved you since the first day I met you by the birch trees on your family's property. And that won't ever change," he said, rubbing his thumb across her cheek. He leaned down and placed his lips on hers, hoping to show her with this triumphant kiss that he meant every word he was saying.

"I can't believe this is happening," she said, shaking her head. "I hoped you would feel this way because I love you too, Deacon. And I've been bursting to tell you, but I totally lost my nerve."

"I get it. I was closed off to speaking up myself. Our road to love has been full of so many twists and turns," Deacon said. Sometimes it seemed as if they had been fighting for their love since the day they met. At this point, he knew that he would always fight for their happily-ever-after. What they felt for one another was worth it. Love everlasting.

Violet reached up and slipped her arms around his neck, looking deeply into his eyes. What she saw shining back at her was everything she'd ever wanted from the love of her life. She saw the promise of forever.

"You've been through so much, Deacon, yet you've emerged as a strong man of faith. You're an amazing father. And the way you love me leaves me awestruck."

"I'm the man I am because of you, Violet, and all the love you've given me. I held on to that when I was in witness protection. That love was a lifeline." He traced the outline of her lips with his finger. "My heart has always belonged to you. And it always will.

"It's taken me a long time, but I've finally found my way home, Violet. Back to you. Back to us."

She laced her fingers through his. "Welcome home, Deacon. We love you. I want nothing more than to walk through life with you by my side."

"We've got a lot of living to do," he said, dipping his head down and pressing another kiss on her lips. "And there's nothing that can separate us this time around."

"Nobody and nothing," she agreed before losing herself in a kiss that signified their hopes for a brilliant future.

Epilogue

"A little rain is supposed to bring a bride good fortune," Skye said as she adjusted the hem of Violet's wedding dress.

"Well that's good," Violet said, peering outside her window at the rain pouring down in buckets. "Because this looks like a tsunami."

But it didn't bother her at all. Nothing could dampen her spirits today, least of all a little rain storm. She was over the moon with happiness about finally walking down the aisle with the man of her dreams. Their joy had been a decade in the making, with so many obstacles thrown in their path. In the end, love had prevailed.

"Mom would be so proud of you, Violet," Skye said, blinking back tears.

"I wish she was here, but I know she's watching over me," Violet said, dabbing at her eyes with her finger.

Skye embraced her, saying, "She is. Always."

In many ways, Violet felt as if she had been waiting her entire life for this incredible moment. Today was the culmination of so many hopes and dreams. She couldn't imagine the day unfolding any more beautifully. She was wearing her mother's vintage wedding gown, one that had been in her family for generations. Chantilly lace with mulberry silk, the gown had a high neckline and delicate embellishments that gave it a regal look. She wasn't used to feeling elegant, but she'd never felt more graceful in her life. She could feel her mother's presence all around her.

Her father appeared in the doorway, tapping his watch. "It's time to go. You are one beautiful bride. The very image of your mother."

Knowing that her parents' love story was still in full bloom reminded Violet of the enduring nature of love. Although wedding vows stated "till death do us part," even death hadn't ended Abel's love for Sugar.

When they reached Serenity Church, Violet let out a gasp as the rain stopped and the sun broke through the clouds. She felt as if God was sending her a signal right before she entered the church.

"Look at that," Abel said, pointing up at the sky. "The sun is coming out just for you and Deacon."

"Hallelujah," Violet said, raising her hand in the air.

As the car door swung open, her father was there reaching for her hand and gently helping her step out. Skye held up the train of her dress so it wouldn't get soiled.

Once they were in the bridal suite, Violet, Skye, Autumn and Abel joined hands and prayed for Deacon and Violet's marriage. She knew that Deacon's faith was as important to him as her own was to her. God had been right beside him throughout his trials, lifting him up and showing him the way out of the darkness. Violet knew that faith would be a strong foundation for their life together.

Autumn and Skye preceded her as her matrons of honor, and then it was time for her to go.

"Ready?" her father asked her as she looped her arm through his. She nodded, and he began to walk her down the aisle. Violet inhaled a deep breath as the strains of the wedding march reached her ears.

Tears sprang to her eyes when she spotted Deacon standing at the altar in a black tuxedo with Chase at his side as best man. They looked identical in their matching suits and pink boutonnieres. Her husband to be looked swoon-worthy.

Everyone she cared about was here, showering her and Deacon with love. His family had even traveled from Chicago to offer their support and blessings for their new life together. Seeing Deacon and his father together had been a poignant moment. Deacon had already pledged to take her and Chase to Chicago during Sugar Works' off-season so that they could get to know his family. But he'd made it clear that Serenity Peak was where he wanted to plant roots.

As they reached the altar, her father leaned in and placed a kiss on her temple before releasing her arm and taking a seat in the front pew.

"You look stunning," Deacon said, reaching for her hand and raising it to his lips. "My beautiful Violet."

"You clean up pretty nicely yourself," Violet said, grinning. She looked over at Chase and gave him a thumbs-up. Their son had never looked happier. His smile was an ear-to-ear grin that dominated his face. He was over-the-moon excited about his parents tying the knot. According to Chase, he'd prayed about it coming to pass.

As they exchanged their vows and pledged to be with one another for the rest of their lives, both of them gave way to the emotion of the moment. They had been through so much, and despite all the odds against them, here they stood, stronger than they'd ever been.

"I do," they murmured as they placed gold rings on each other's fingers and exchanged a tender kiss. The guests clapped loudly and let out whistles of approval.

"I can't believe you're finally my wife," Deacon said, grasping her hand in his and heading back toward the front of the church. "A long-held dream come true."

"Woot! We really did it," Violet said, letting out a little squeal. What she was feeling right now was unlike anything she had ever before experienced. She wished that she could capture this moment in a bottle and savor it for all time. This type of joy hummed and pulsed in the air around them, spreading to all their family and friends. It was effusive. She couldn't explain why, but the sun shone brighter and the sky was as vivid as a robin's egg. Everything had fallen perfectly into place, exceeding all of her most cherished dreams.

As soon as they stepped outside the church, they were inundated with handfuls of birdseed being thrown over their heads. They stood in a receiving line and accepted well wishes from all of those near and dear to them.

Skye hugged Violet tightly, promising to look after Chase while they were away.

A Just Married sign hung on the bumper of the white Bentley that was going to whisk them to a seaplane. They were flying to Sitka for their honeymoon. Her heart was full to overflowing with love. She almost wanted to pinch herself to make sure she wasn't dreaming. Nothing about her love story had been perfect other than their wedding day.

Deacon swung the car door open and held the hem of her gown as she stepped inside. Chase and a few of his friends ran after the car as it drove off, waving and shouting. Violet waved back and wiped away the stray tears on her cheeks.

"Hey, my love, no more tears," Deacon said, dipping his head down to place a kiss on her lips. "From this moment forward, we're going to spend every moment in pure bliss."

Her husband was right. There was no place for tears now. The darkness was part of their past. There was nothing but bright skies ahead. And memories to be made.

Life was good. Deacon was her true north. After all, he'd found his way back to her and their son after so much tumult. And from here on out, he would never be far away from her, Chase or this town he now called his own.

* * * * *

If you enjoyed this story,
check out Skye and Ryan's story,
An Alaskan Blessing,
by Belle Calhoune!

Available now from Love Inspired.
And discover more at
LoveInspired.com.

Dear Reader,

Thank you so much for joining me on another Serenity Peak adventure. Violet and Deacon's love story has been a pleasure to write, although a bit emotional for me. Deacon is a man who has lost so much, yet he continues to make positive strides to rebuild his life. Violet is dealing with the shock of her ex-fiancé's return and learning about his involvement in witness protection. At the same time, they are both trying to protect Chase. I think both of them are very courageous in confronting the past while remaining grounded in the present.

Starting over and forgiveness are two themes that resonate throughout the book. In order to fully embrace the future, Deacon and Violet must lay the past to rest. Deacon has had a lot of pain in his life, so he definitely deserves a happy ending with Violet and Chase.

As always, it's an honor to write for

Harlequin Love Inspired. In fact, this is my twentieth book for the line. It's definitely something to celebrate. You can find me online at my Author Belle Calhoune Facebook page or sign up for my newsletter via my bellecalhoune.com website.

Blessings,
Belle